PENGUIN CI

JOHN BUCHAN was born in Perth in 1875. His father was a minister of the Free Church of Scotland; and in 1876 the family moved to Fife, where John walked six miles a day to school. Later they moved to Glasgow and, when he went to Glasgow University, he published articles in periodicals. When at Brasenose College, Oxford, he published five books and many articles, and won several awards, including the Newdigate Prize for poetry. His career was diverse and successful, and despite ill health, he was a barrister and Member of Parliament, in addition to being a writer, soldier and publisher. He married, and had four children. He was created Baron Tweedsmuir of Elsfield in 1935 and became the Governor-General of Canada, until his death in 1940.

His first success as an author came with *Prester John* in 1910, and he went on to write a series of adventure thrillers, or 'shockers' as he called them, all characterized by their authentically rendered backgrounds, romantic characters, their atmosphere of expectancy and world-wide conspiracies, and the author's own enthusiasm. His main heroes were Richard Hannay in *The Thirty-Nine Steps* and four other books, Dickson McCunn, the Glaswegian provision merchant with the soul of a romantic, and Edward Leithen, eminent lawyer. Buchan also established a reputation as an historical biographer with such works as *Montrose*, *Oliver Cromwell* and *Augustus*.

SIR JOHN KEEGAN is a military historian and the author of twenty books, including *The Face of Battle*, *The Mask of Command* and *The First World War*. He was the Reith Lecturer in 1998 and is an Honorary Fellow of Balliol College, Oxford.

WITHDRAWN FROM STOCK

JOHN BUCHAN

The Thirty-Nine Steps

With an Introduction and Notes by
SIR JOHN KEEGAN

PENGUIN BOOKS

PENGUIN BOOKS

Published by the Penguin Group
Penguin Books Ltd, 80 Strand, London WC2R ORL, England
Penguin Group (USA) Inc., 375 Hudson Street, New York, New York 10014, USA
Penguin Books Australia Ltd, 250 Camberwell Road, Camberwell, Victoria 3124, Australia
Penguin Books Canada Ltd, 10 Alcorn Avenue, Toronto, Ontario, Canada M4V 3B2
Penguin Books India (P) Ltd, 11, Community Centre, Panchsheel Park, New Delhi – 110 017, India
Penguin Books (NZ) Ltd, Cnr Rosedale and Airborne Roads, Albany, Auckland, New Zealand
Penguin Books (South Africa) (Pty) Ltd, 24 Sturdee Avenue, Rosebank 2196, South Africa

Penguin Books Ltd, Registered Offices: 80 Strand, London WC2R ORL, England

www.penguin.com

First published 1915
This edition published in Penguin Classics 2004

12

Editorial material copyright © Sir John Keegan, 2004
All rights reserved

Set in 10.25/12.25 pt PostScript Adobe Sabon
Typeset by Rowland Phototypesetting Ltd, Bury St Edmunds, Suffolk
Printed in England by Clays Ltd, St Ives plc

ISBN-13: 978–0–141–44117–7

www.greenpenguin.co.uk

Contents

Chronology

1875 26 *August*: born in Perth, the eldest son of a Free Church of Scotland Minister.

1876 Buchan family moves to Fife.

1888 Family moves to Glasgow.

1888–92 Attends Hutcheson's Grammar School, Glasgow.

1892–5 First degree at Glasgow University.

1895 *Don Quixote of the Moors*, Buchan's first adventure story, published.

1895–9 At Brasenose Collge, Oxford. Wins the Newdigate Prize in Poetry (1898). President of the Oxford Union in his final year. Achieves a first-class degree in Greats in 1899.

1901 Called to the Bar but did not practise as a barrister.

1901–3 In South Africa. Private secretary to Lord Milner, High Commissioner for South Africa.

1906 Joins Nelson publishers.

1907 Marries Susan Grosvenor; they have three sons and one daughter.

1908 First child, Alice, born.

1910 Publication of *Prester John*.

1911 Publication of *Sir Walter Raleigh* biography.

1914 Begins to write *The Thirty-Nine Steps* while ill in bed during the first months of the war.

1915 Publication of *The Thirty-Nine Steps*, the first of the five Richard Hannay novels. Works as a journalist attached to the British Army in France, writing for *The Times* and the *Daily News*, covering the second Battle of Ypres and the Battle of Loos.

1916 Publication of *Greenmantle* (a Hannay novel) and of *The*

Power House, the first of three novels featuring Barrister Sir Edward Leithen. Son William born. Appointed Second Lieutenant in the Intelligence Corps.

1917 Appointed Director of Information for the government. Brother Alastair and friend Tommy Nelson killed on the Western Front.

1919 Publication of *Mr Standfast* (a Hannay novel). Buys Elsfield Manor, Oxfordshire. Becomes a director of the news agency Reuters.

1921 Publication of *Huntingtower*, the first of three novels featuring the hero Dickson McCunn, a retired Glasgow provisions merchant.

1924 Publication of *The Three Hostages* (a Hannay novel).

1925 Publication of *John MacNab* (a Leithen novel).

1927 Elected Member of Parliament (Conservative) for the Scottish Universities.

1929–32 Appointed President of the Scottish History Society.

1930 Publication of *Castle Gray* (a McCunn novel).

1932 Appointed Companion of Honour.

1933–4 Appointed Lord High Commissioner to the General Assembly of the Church of Scotland.

1935 Publication of *House of the Four Winds* (a McCunn novel). Alfred Hitchcock film of *The Thirty-Nine Steps* released. Appointed Governor-General of Canada and created Baron Tweedsmuir.

1936 Publication of *The Island of Sheep* (*Man from the Norlands*) (a Hannay novel).

1937 Elected Chancellor of Edinburgh University and made Privy Councillor. Mother, Helen Buchan, dies.

1939 Appointed GCVO (Knight Grand Cross of the Royal Victorian Order).

1940 *12 February*: dies in Montreal.

1941 Posthumous publication of *Sick Heart River* (*Mountain Meadow*) (a Leithen novel).

Introduction

'It was one of those days,' a friend said, 'when the only thing to do was read John Buchan.' I knew at once what was meant. We all know days when the small irritations of life conspire to prevent one settling to anything. There is work to be done but no motivation, arrangements to be made but no impulse. Letters lie accusingly unanswered. A vague sense of unease pervades one's being. An inner voice tells one to snap out of it. The will to alter one's mood is inexplicably absent.

There is a very English recipe for dealing with this condition – fresh air, physical exercise, direct contact with nature. Getting out of oneself is the cure, particularly to hills, cliffs, high tops, where the turf is springy and the views stretch to distant, blue horizons. Oppressive days come, however, when such escapes may not offer. City streets and crowds surround, unyielding pavements meet one's feet, horizons can only be imagined. At such times, Buchan opens the door to the world one's being seeks – a world of thickets refreshed by a recent rain shower, of streams tinkling over boulders smoothed by uncountable winter floods, of the sharp cry of an unseen bird in a bush, of peat smoke rising lazily from a cottage chimney in the calm evening air, a world of nature utterly at peace and yet – here is the key Buchan ingredient – tinged with the menace of man the enemy.

Buchan knew the landscapes he describes so evocatively – they are usually Scottish, not English – because he took his greatest pleasure, all his life, in walking the country ways and scrambling in high places. He fished, he watched birds, he learned the names of the wild plants and as he grew older he read the history and legends of lowland and highland, feeding his vivid imagination on stories of border raids, clan feuds and Jacobite adventure. The longer the walk, the harder the climb, the more he enjoyed the holiday. He took little with him, fed on oatcakes, sometimes slept in the open under a plaid, swam at daybreak in the waters of a loch, found shelter at night with a friendly crofter. Companions of the road, drovers, shepherds, hill farmers on the way to market, fed his store of dialect tales and folk wisdom. Distance and remoteness entered his being.

Yet Buchan was not really a countryman. His hills, dales, gentle riversides and tinkling burns were brilliantly created products of his imagination rather than images of daily experience. His childhood was spent in a small town, where his Free Church of Scotland father began his ministry, his youth in the narrow streets of Glasgow. Even in his early years, the countryside was a place of escape, not a defining environment. It was for that reason that it worked so powerfully on his consciousness. Real countrymen are less romantic about their surroundings. Buchan the author conveys the magic of nature as successfully as he does because nature was for him an experience of time spent away from home, not of home itself.

John Buchan, born on 26 August 1875, was the son of William Buchan, clergyman, and Helen Masterson, a sheep farmer's daughter, only just eighteen at the time of the birth of her first child. The family were modestly middle class, a status Buchan would never deny, even when fame and fortune carried him into the ranks of the rich and great. He began his education at the local board school. When his father was appointed to a large Free Church parish in the Gorbals, he transferred to Hutcheson's, a Glasgow grammar school. Later, with sons at Eton, he would say, 'I never went to school in the conventional sense' but the truth was that schools like Hutcheson's were the normal destination of boys of the Scottish middle class. Hutcheson's, moreover, did him well. He won a scholarship that paid his fees of four guineas a year and in 1892, aged sixteen, a bursary to Glasgow University.

Scottish universities, in Buchan's youth, were to Oxford and Cambridge as Hutcheson's was to an English public school –

hard-scrabble places of study, not seminaries for young gentlemen. Glasgow University in the 1890s, however, had several
professors who came from Oxford or Cambridge or were going
on to chairs there. As Buchan's university years extended, and
he took the measure of his talents, the idea grew of trying
for Oxford himself. The expense, which might have been an
insuperable obstacle, he was equipped to meet because he
had already begun to write for money. With remarkable self-
confidence he tried stories and essays on Scottish and English
magazines and won acceptances; he went to see editors and so
impressed that he was taken on to read the manuscripts of other
would-be writers. When, in 1895, he went up to Oxford, he was
earning £70 a year by writing and the further expenses of his
first year were just covered by a scholarship he won. Four
years later his annual income was over £400, £130 from his
scholarship, the rest from publishers. He was much better off
than most middle-class undergraduates and no charge on his
father.

Oxford did more than start Buchan on his literary career. It
also launched him into English life. Buchan never ceased to be
a Scot, then or later, but he did not insist on his Scottishness, as
many fellow countrymen abroad did. Within a year of leaving
Glasgow, his Scottish accent had almost disappeared and, by
the time he left Oxford, his close friends were almost all English,
many, such as Raymond Asquith, from leading English families.
He moved, moreover, in English society without any unease or
self-consciousness. His transition from teenage Glasgow gradu-
ate to young man-about-town in London was achieved with
apparently effortless smoothness.

Propulsion rather than escalation was the secret. Buchan
stood out, even as an undergraduate, but did not obtrude or
impose. He was liked by his contemporaries and admired. They
foresaw for him a great future, in politics, the law or public life.
Not without reason. He had appeared in *Who's Who* at the age
of twenty-three, been published in the *Yellow Book*, been elected
President of the Union and, in his last term, achieved a First in
Greats. His friends not only expected him to succeed but wished
and helped him to do so.

His early career bore out his early promise. Deciding to go to the bar, he quickly found chambers and was called as a barrister, after one failed attempt at the examination, in 1901. It was not his first exam failure; he had also – twice – failed the examination for an All Souls Fellowship. He did not harbour long regrets, recognizing that he was not a natural academic and that life in the great world would suit him better than that of the quadrangle and library. At the bar he continued to write, beginning to turn out journalism for the national papers at a rapid pace and embarking on a full-length novel, through themes developed in his early stories of Scottish adventure and historical romance.

His start in journalism and the law was soon interrupted, however, by a call from afar. In 1901 the Boer War was drawing to a close but the 'bitter enders' among the Boers were refusing to give up. Formal operations were at an end but guerrilla warfare continued in the Transvaal and sporadically in the Orange Free State and even in the British Cape Province. Its effect on the life of the territories was disastrous. The Afrikaners who had surrendered were prisoners, those who had not were fugitives on the veld, farms everywhere were derelict, the Boer women and children were left without proper livelihood. The British solution was to confine them in what were unfortunately called Concentration Camps, where they could be fed but also prevented from supporting their men folk. The intention was benevolent as well as strategic but the result was deplorable. Epidemics broke out in the camps, causing death rates as high as 30 per cent.

There was public outrage and the demand for action. The British government, which had resumed control of the Free State and Transvaal as colonies, had already recognized the need for a programme of reconstruction. Alfred Milner, a leading public servant, High Commissioner for South Africa since 1897, was charged with that duty. His response was to recruit personal secretaries who could carry out the mission. This 'Kindergarten' was to contain some of the most promising young men of their generation, including a future editor of The Times, Geoffrey Dawson, and John Buchan.

Buchan was given two responsibilities: first, to make the

camps healthy; second, to begin reviving agriculture. He did not solve the camp problem; that was done by bringing doctors and nurses experienced in quelling epidemic from Britain and India. His agricultural work was more constructive and, to him, more fulfilling. He liked the Boer farmers, who reminded him of the Border farmers of his childhood. He was at home with their Calvinism, so similar to his own Presbyterianism. Above all, he loved the South African landscape, the far horizons of the high veld, the green slopes of the Magaliesberg range, the tiny woods and valleys of the Drakensberg. He got to know it well, riding long distances across country, discovering places of secret beauty and forming the intention of returning one day to build a house in the wilderness.

He also got to know people he would not have met in his respectable life at the English bar: soldiers, adventurers and men out to make their fortunes in the world. The gold and diamonds of South Africa had attracted fortune-hunters from all over the world who made Johannesburg a cosmopolitan and vibrant city. Many of the adventurers were reasonably law-abiding. Some were not. Buchan found the crooks as interesting as his own sort of high-minded empire builder and was to populate his future novels with characters drawn from his Johannesburg experience.

When he left South Africa at the beginning of 1903, his career as a writer, however, still lay ahead of him. He had published four slight novels and several collections of short stories but he had decided against setting up as a full-time man of letters. Literature was to be 'my hobby, not my profession'; so he summed up his intentions at that time. On returning to London, he resumed his journalism, his legal work, though in chambers, not at court, and sought election to parliament, as a moderate Conservative. He was busy, well known in London society and financially comfortable. After the glitter of his Oxford years, however, and of his first appearance on the literary scene, his career had fallen into eclipse. His early promise had faded, he had ascended no higher the slopes of achievement he seemed destined to conquer. The most notable event of these Edwardian years was his marriage in July 1907 to Susan

Grosvenor. She was everything his doting mother least sought in a bride for her adored eldest son. She was English, Anglican and, by Mrs Buchan's homely standards, a sight too grand, the granddaughter of a peer and a cousin of the Duke of Westminster. She was nevertheless to prove a partner in a happy marriage, though to it she brought no money. John and Susan's growing family would have to be supported by his efforts alone.

The basis of his livelihood as a married man was supplied by his appointment as a partner in the old Edinburgh firm of Thomas Nelson, who had published Walter Scott, Buchan's literary hero. Tommy Nelson, the current head of the firm, was an Oxford contemporary and he and Buchan agreed on a salary of £1,500 a year, a very generous income at the period. More income was welcome, however, for Buchan contributed to the expenses of his parents and his sister, Anna, then setting out herself on the career of a novelist.

So Buchan persisted with his writing. The pattern was much as before: collections of short stories, a novel (*Prester John*) which drew both on Scottish scenes and his African experience, and a biography of the Covenanter Chief, Montrose. None sold more than 2,000 copies and he earned good reviews but little cash.

Then his luck turned. Buchan was prone to exhaustion, as highly strung men who work too hard often are. Moreover he 'relaxed' by taking up a new writing task. In 1913 he had spent his time on a cruise to the Azores composing a 'shocker', which would appear in 1916 as *The Power House*. In the later summer of 1914, as war engulfed Europe, he fell ill again and was taken by Susan to Broadstairs for a holiday. Also holidaying in Broadstairs was a cousin of Susan's, who was renting a clifftop house with steps down to a private beach. As he recuperated, Buchan began his second 'shocker'. He was to call it *The Thirty-Nine Steps*. It was an immediate success when first published in 1915; by 1960 his biographer Janet Adam Smith calculated its sales had reached 355,000 copies. By now the figure is far higher.

It is wrong for an introduction to spoil a reader's enjoyment of the book that follows by revealing anything of its plot. Without doing so, it is possible to say that *The Thirty-Nine Steps* reworks in literary form much of Buchan's life thus far (he was thirty-nine in August 1914). The beginning of the action is set in Scotland, at first in Galloway, which he knew well from a long Oxford holiday, then in Upper Tweeddale. He peoples the action with Scottish types met during childhood stays in Tweeddale or on his student tramps around the Lowlands. The prologue, however, is staged in London, the London of clubs and West End streets in which he settled after arriving in the capital, and the atmosphere of a rich, complacent imperial city is perfectly caught in his description of how a returned colonial, his hero Richard Hannay, swiftly tires of the allurements of metropolitan life.

After Hannay's adventure in Scotland, the action shifts to the Thames Valley, a countryside of sleepy villages and peaceful trout streams, explored during Buchan's years at Oxford, and then quite unspoiled by the extension of London's tentacles into its water meadows and chalk downland. The Thames Valley remained as rural as it had been when Gray was writing the *Elegy in a Country Churchyard* and the only outsiders were grandees rich enough to build weekend retreats. Buchan captures the type and the atmosphere to perfection in his depiction of Sir Walter Bullivant, the government insider and man of secrets.

The culmination of the plot carries Richard Hannay, after a second London episode, to the Channel coast. As he wrote the final chapters, Buchan was drawing directly on the scenes that lay about him during his recuperation in Broadstairs. His evocation of monied leisure at the early twentieth-century seaside could not be bettered. The description of beach donkeys and pierrots padding homeward in the warm twilight past the garden gates of comfortable villas, where maids wait to serve supper and the hall tables are covered with tennis rackets and folded waterproofs, perfectly conveys the sense of a privileged class enjoying its release from city labour among locals with real breadwinning to do. Buchan was by then one of the privileged; but he was not far enough away from the Gorbals to disguise his knowledge of the realities of the breadwinning world of his childhood.

Most realistic of all is his characterization of his hero, Richard Hannay. Hannay, perhaps inevitably, is a Scot, and a Scot who has made his way in the world. Buchan knew about self-made Scots, but Hannay is also a colonial, a type he knew only from the outside. One of the triumphs of *The Thirty-Nine Steps* is Buchan's realization of an exile who has made a pile in a harsh world and returned to the motherland to enjoy what he has won. The frustrated energy, the impatience with convention, but also the fundamental deference towards Imperial Britain's great and good ring absolutely true. So too does Hannay's personal integrity. He may look up to grandees, whom his adventure brings him to meet with surprising frequency. At his centre, however, Hannay believes in himself, as a successful professional – his pile was made as a mining engineer – and in his own simple but unswerving code of right and wrong. Moral certainty, which Buchan possessed in abundance, was one of his strengths as a writer. It gave him the power to achieve something particularly elusive: moral atmosphere.

The Thirty-Nine Steps is not, however its author described it, merely a 'shocker'. It is a story of good and evil. Given Buchan's optimistic and forgiving nature, he could not make the evil very severe. His villains are not beyond redemption and what they plot is less than diabolical. The good, by contrast, is very good indeed. That is what makes his world and his heroes so attractive. They are upright and chivalrous, as well as unthinkingly brave, and they enjoy the sublime assurance that, when things look at their blackest, chance will cast them in the path of someone ready to help who is just like themselves. The Buchan firmament is peopled by characters who are instinctively patriotic, romantically unselfish and ready at a moment's notice to abandon everyday duty to do service to the cause.

Buchan's 'cause' was by no means as simple as King and Country, deeply loyal though he was to both. It partook also of Scottishness, the Scotland of burn and bracken but also of the One True Kirk, and anomalously of England as well, an idealized England of high-minded gentlemen and idyllic landscape. There were other elements, including a strong populism – Buchan's humbler folk exude sturdy virtue – a pervasive respect for institutions and a whiff of Empire. Suffusing everything is something distinctively Buchanesque, a hint of presences just beyond the boundary of consciousness. Buchan's world, and the values for which his characters are ready to risk their lives, is utterly matter-of-fact; but at its fringe hover unseen, undefined powers whose intervention can never be discounted.

It is the dimension of the mysterious that makes Buchan's writing so unfailingly compelling. It is the other ingredients – strong characters, often if minor participants drawn with brilliant comedy, exact and evocative scene-setting, highly authentic dialogue, particularly if rendered in dialect, sudden surprises and, above all, rapid change of location – that make him so readable. Buchan is a master of pace. Raymond Chandler, one of his admirers, laid down the principle that the mystery writer, if in doubt as to how to proceed, should have a man come through a door with a gun in his hand. Buchan never seems in any doubt as to how to proceed; but he sustains interest by the relentless speed with which he shifts scenes. Hannay's rush from London to Galloway to the Highlands to the Thames Valley to London again and finally to the Channel coast, by express train, high-powered motor car and on his own fleet feet, leaves the reader breathless, but also panting to know what lies beyond the next twist in the plot.

It does not disappoint. Better than that, the narrative is deeply satisfying. Buchan had a happy and wonderful life, culminating in his appointment, as Lord Tweedsmuir, to be Governor-General of Canada. His personal saga was already launched when he began *The Thirty-Nine Steps*. Its consistently optimistic mood and its simple theme of the triumph of a good man over his country's enemies reflect the story of his own life thus far and anticipate its development. If Hannay's succession of chance encounters with humble helpmates and powerful supporters, wholly unlikely though it may be, rings true, it is because Buchan was drawing on his own lucky experiences.

John Buchan was blessed by fortune, which brought a Scottish boy of obscure family to fame, wealth and lifelong friendship with the greatest in the land. He deserved every particle of his success, for he was a writer touched by genius. The outline of his enormous talent is discernible in each page of *The Thirty-Nine Steps*.

Further Reading

John Buchan published over a hundred books, most of them written by himself but including some edited collections. There is a bibliography of his works by Archibald Hanna (Shoestring Press, 1953). Important biographical or critical works include:

Adam Smith, Janet, *John Buchan* (London, 1965).
Buchan, Susan, *John Buchan by His Wife and Friends* (London, 1947).
Buchan, William, *John Buchan: A Memoir* (London, 1982).
Lowrie, Andrew, *John Buchan, The Presbyterian Cavalier* (London, 1995).
Usborne, Richard, *Clubland Heroes* (London, 1953 and 1974).
Webb, Paul, *A Buchan Companion* (London, 1994).

John Buchan's autobiography, *Memory-Hold-The-Door*, written while he was Governor-General of Canada, was published posthumously in 1940.

A Note on The Text

The text is the first edition, published by William Blackwood and Sons, London and Edinburgh, 1915. House styling has been applied to punctuation, e.g. quotation marks (doubles have become singles) and dashes (unspaced M-dashes to spaced N).

Two German words have been corrected: *Der Schwarzestein* (p. 113) from *Der Schwarzstein* and 'Marineamt' (p. 83) from 'Marinamt'.

The Thirty-Nine Steps

Contents

CHAPTER I
THE MAN WHO DIED

I returned from the City about three o'clock on that May afternoon pretty well disgusted with life. I had been three months in
the Old Country, and was fed up with it. If any one had told me
a year ago that I would have been feeling like that I should have
laughed at him; but there was the fact. The weather made me
liverish, the talk of the ordinary Englishman made me sick, I
couldn't get enough exercise, and the amusements of London
seemed as flat as soda-water that has been standing in the sun.
'Richard Hannay,' I kept telling myself, 'you have got into the
wrong ditch, my friend, and you had better climb out.'

It made me bite my lips to think of the plans I had been
building up those last years in Buluwayo.[1] I had got my pile –
not one of the big ones, but good enough for me; and I had
figured out all kinds of ways of enjoying myself. My father had
brought me out from Scotland at the age of six, and I had never
been home since; so England was a sort of Arabian Nights to
me, and I counted on stopping there for the rest of my days.

But from the first I was disappointed with it. In about a week
I was tired of seeing sights, and in less than a month I had had
enough of restaurants and theatres and race-meetings. I had no
real pal to go about with, which probably explains things. Plenty
of people invited me to their houses, but they didn't seem much
interested in me. They would fling me a question or two about
South Africa, and then get on to their own affairs. A lot of
Imperialist ladies asked me to tea to meet schoolmasters from
New Zealand and editors from Vancouver, and that was the
dismalest business of all. Here was I, thirty-seven years old,
sound in wind and limb, with enough money to have a good

time, yawning my head off all day. I had just about settled to clear out and get back to the veld, for I was the best bored man in the United Kingdom.

That afternoon I had been worrying my brokers about investments to give my mind something to work on, and on my way home I turned into my club – rather a pot-house,[2] which took in Colonial members. I had a long drink, and read the evening papers. They were full of the row in the Near East, and there was an article about Karolides, the Greek Premier. I rather fancied the chap. From all accounts he seemed the one big man in the show; and he played a straight game too, which was more than could be said for most of them. I gathered that they hated him pretty blackly in Berlin and Vienna, but that we were going to stick by him, and one paper said that he was the only barrier between Europe and Armageddon. I remember wondering if I could get a job in those parts. It struck me that Albania was the sort of place that might keep a man from yawning.

About six o'clock I went home, dressed, dined at the Café Royal, and turned into a music-hall. It was a silly show, all capering women and monkey-faced men, and I did not stay long. The night was fine and clear as I walked back to the flat I had hired near Portland Place. The crowd surged past me on the pavements, busy and chattering, and I envied the people for having something to do. These shop-girls and clerks and dandies and policemen had some interest in life that kept them going. I gave half-a-crown to a beggar because I saw him yawn; he was a fellow-sufferer. At Oxford Circus I looked up into the spring sky and I made a vow. I would give the Old Country another day to fit me into something; if nothing happened, I would take the next boat for the Cape.[3]

My flat was the first floor in a new block behind Langham Place.[4] There was a common staircase, with a porter and a liftman at the entrance, but there was no restaurant or anything of that sort, and each flat was quite shut off from the others. I hate servants on the premises, so I had a fellow to look after me who came in by the day. He arrived before eight o'clock every morning and used to depart at seven, for I never dined at home.

I was just fitting my key into the door when I noticed a man at my elbow. I had not seen him approach, and the sudden appearance made me start. He was a slim man, with a short brown beard and small, gimlety blue eyes. I recognised him as the occupant of a flat on the top floor, with whom I had passed the time of day on the stairs.

'Can I speak to you?' he said. 'May I come in for a minute?' He was steadying his voice with an effort, and his hand was pawing my arm.

I got my door open and motioned him in. No sooner was he over the threshold than he made a dash for my back-room, where I used to smoke and write my letters. Then he bolted back.

'Is the door locked?' he asked feverishly, and he fastened the chain with his own hand.

'I'm very sorry,' he said humbly. 'It's a mighty liberty, but you looked the kind of man who would understand. I've had you in my mind all this week when things got troublesome. Say, will you do me a good turn?'

'I'll listen to you,' I said. 'That's all I'll promise.' I was getting worried by the antics of this nervous little chap.

There was a tray of drinks on a table beside him, from which he filled himself a stiff whisky-and-soda. He drank it off in three gulps, and cracked the glass as he set it down.

'Pardon,' he said, 'I'm a bit rattled to-night. You see, I happen at this moment to be dead.'

I sat down in an arm-chair and lit my pipe.

'What does it feel like?' I asked. I was pretty certain that I had to deal with a madman.

A smile flickered over his drawn face. 'I'm not mad – yet. Say, sir, I've been watching you, and I reckon you're a cool customer. I reckon, too, you're an honest man, and not afraid of playing a bold hand. I'm going to confide in you. I need help worse than any man ever needed it, and I want to know if I can count you in.'

'Get on with your yarn,' I said, 'and I'll tell you.'

He seemed to brace himself for a great effort, and then started on the queerest rigmarole. I didn't get hold of it at first, and I had to stop and ask him questions. But here is the gist of it:–

He was an American, from Kentucky, and after college, being pretty well off, he had started out to see the world. He wrote a bit, and acted as war correspondent for a Chicago paper, and spent a year or two in South-Eastern Europe. I gathered that he was a fine linguist, and had got to know pretty well the society in those parts. He spoke familiarly of many names that I remembered to have seen in the newspapers.

He had played about with politics, he told me, at first for the interest of them, and then because he couldn't help himself. I read him as a sharp, restless fellow, who always wanted to get down to the roots of things. He got a little further down than he wanted.

I am giving you what he told me as well as I could make it out. Away behind all the Governments and the armies there was a big subterranean movement going on, engineered by very dangerous people. He had come on it by accident; it fascinated him; he went further, and then he got caught. I gathered that most of the people in it were the sort of educated anarchists that make revolutions, but that beside them there were financiers who were playing for money. A clever man can make big profits on a falling market, and it suited the book of both classes to set Europe by the ears.

He told me some queer things that explained a lot that had puzzled me – things that happened in the Balkan War,[5] how one state suddenly came out on top, why alliances were made and broken, why certain men disappeared, and where the sinews of war came from. The aim of the whole conspiracy was to get Russia and Germany at loggerheads.

When I asked Why, he said that the anarchist lot thought it would give them their chance. Everything would be in the melting-pot, and they looked to see a new world emerge. The capitalists would rake in the shekels, and make fortunes by buying up wreckage. Capital, he said, had no conscience and no fatherland. Besides, the Jew was behind it, and the Jew hated Russia worse than hell.

'Do you wonder?' he cried. 'For three hundred years they have been persecuted, and this is the return match for the *pogroms*.[6] The Jew is everywhere, but you have to go far down

the backstairs to find him. Take any big Teutonic business
concern. If you have dealings with it the first man you meet is
Prince *von und zu* Something, an elegant young man who talks
Eton-and-Harrow English. But he cuts no ice. If your business
is big, you get behind him and find a prognathous Westphalian
with a retreating brow and the manners of a hog. He is the
German business man that gives your English papers the shakes.
But if you're on the biggest kind of job and are bound to get to
the real boss, ten to one you are brought up against a little
white-faced Jew in a bath-chair with an eye like a rattlesnake.
Yes, sir, he is the man who is ruling the world just now, and he
has his knife in the Empire of the Tzar, because his aunt was
outraged and his father flogged in some one-horse location on
the Volga.'

I could not help saying that his Jew-anarchists seemed to have
got left behind a little.

'Yes and no,' he said. 'They won up to a point, but they struck
a bigger thing than money, a thing that couldn't be bought, the
old elemental fighting instincts of man. If you're going to be
killed you invent some kind of flag and country to fight for, and
if you survive you get to love the thing. Those foolish devils of
soldiers have found something they care for, and that has upset
the pretty plan laid in Berlin and Vienna. But my friends haven't
played their last card by a long sight. They've gotten the ace up
their sleeves, and unless I can keep alive for a month they are
going to play it and win.'

'But I thought you were dead,' I put in.

'*Mors janua vitae*,'[7] he smiled. (I recognised the quotation: it
was about all the Latin I knew.) 'I'm coming to that, but I've
got to put you wise about a lot of things first. If you read
your newspaper, I guess you know the name of Constantine
Karolides?'

I sat up at that, for I had been reading about him that very
afternoon.

'He is the man that has wrecked all their games. He is the one
big brain in the whole show, and he happens also to be an
honest man. Therefore he has been marked down these twelve
months past. I found that out – not that it was difficult, for any

fool could guess as much. But I found out the way they were going to get him, and that knowledge was deadly. That's why I have had to decease.'

He had another drink, and I mixed it for him myself, for I was getting interested in the beggar.

'They can't get him in his own land, for he has a bodyguard of Epirotes[8] that would skin their grandmothers. But on the 15th day of June he is coming to this city. The British Foreign Office has taken to having International tea-parties, and the biggest of them is due on that date. Now Karolides is reckoned the principal guest, and if my friends have their way he will never return to his admiring countrymen.'

'That's simple enough, anyhow,' I said. 'You can warn him and keep him at home.'

'And play their game?' he asked sharply. 'If he does not come they win, for he's the only man that can straighten out the tangle. And if his Government are warned he won't come, for he does not know how big the stakes will be on June the 15th.'

'What about the British Government?' I said. 'They're not going to let their guests be murdered. Tip them the wink, and they'll take extra precautions.'

'No good. They might stuff your city with plain-clothes detectives and double the police and Constantine would still be a doomed man. My friends are not playing this game for candy. They want a big occasion for the taking off, with the eyes of all Europe on it. He'll be murdered by an Austrian, and there'll be plenty of evidence to show the connivance of the big folk in Vienna and Berlin. It will all be an infernal lie, of course, but the case will look black enough to the world. I'm not talking hot air, my friend. I happen to know every detail of the hellish contrivance, and I can tell you it will be the most finished piece of blackguardism since the Borgias. But it's not going to come off if there's a certain man who knows the wheels of the business alive right here in London on the 15th day of June. And that man is going to be your servant, Franklin P. Scudder.'

I was getting to like the little chap. His jaw had shut like a rat-trap, and there was the fire of battle in his gimlety eyes. If he was spinning me a yarn he could act up to it.

'Where did you find out this story?' I asked.

'I got the first hint in an inn on the Achensee in Tyrol. That set me inquiring, and I collected my other clues in a fur-shop in the Galician quarter of Buda, in a Strangers' Club in Vienna, and in a little bookshop off the Racknitzstrasse in Leipsic. I completed my evidence ten days ago in Paris. I can't tell you the details now, for it's something of a history. When I was quite sure in my own mind I judged it my business to disappear, and I reached this city by a mighty queer circuit. I left Paris a dandified young French-American, and I sailed from Hamburg a Jew diamond merchant. In Norway I was an English student of Ibsen collecting materials for lectures, but when I left Bergen I was a cinema-man with special ski films. And I came here from Leith with a lot of pulp-wood propositions in my pocket to put before the London newspapers. Till yesterday I thought I had muddied my trail some, and was feeling pretty happy. Then . . .'

The recollection seemed to upset him, and he gulped down some more whisky.

'Then I saw a man standing in the street outside this block. I used to stay close in my room all day, and only slip out after dark for an hour or two. I watched him for a bit from my window, and I thought I recognised him . . . He came in and spoke to the porter . . . When I came back from my walk last night I found a card in my letter-box. It bore the name of the man I want least to meet on God's earth.'

I think that the look in my companion's eyes, the sheer naked scare on his face, completed my conviction of his honesty. My own voice sharpened a bit as I asked him what he did next.

'I realised that I was bottled as sure as a pickled herring, and that there was only one way out. I had to die. If my pursuers knew I was dead they would go to sleep again.'

'How did you manage it?'

'I told the man that valets me that I was feeling pretty bad, and I got myself up to look like death. That wasn't difficult, for I'm no slouch at disguises. Then I got a corpse – you can always get a body in London if you know where to go for it. I fetched it back in a trunk on the top of a four-wheeler,[9] and I had to be

assisted upstairs to my room. You see I had to pile up some
evidence for the inquest. I went to bed and got my man to
mix me a sleeping-draught, and then told him to clear out. He
wanted to fetch a doctor, but I swore some and said I couldn't
abide leeches. When I was left alone I started in to fake up
that corpse. He was my size, and I judged had perished from
too much alcohol, so I put some spirits handy about the place.
The jaw was the weak point in the likeness, so I blew it away
with a revolver. I daresay there will be somebody to-morrow to
swear to having heard a shot, but there are no neighbours on
my floor, and I guessed I could risk it. So I left the body in
bed dressed up in my pyjamas with a revolver lying on the
bed-clothes and a considerable mess around. Then I got into a
suit of clothes I had kept waiting for emergencies. I didn't dare
to shave for fear of leaving tracks, and besides, it wasn't any
kind of use my trying to get into the streets. I had had you in
my mind all day, and there seemed nothing to do but to make
an appeal to you. I watched from my window till I saw you
come home, and then slipped down the stair to meet you . . .
There, sir, I guess you know about as much as me of this
business.'

He sat blinking like an owl, fluttering with nerves and yet
desperately determined. By this time I was pretty well convinced
that he was going straight with me. It was the wildest sort of
narrative, but I had heard in my time many steep tales which
had turned out to be true, and I had made a practice of judging
the man rather than the story. If he had wanted to get a location
in my flat, and then cut my throat, he would have pitched a
milder yarn.

'Hand me your key,' I said, 'and I'll take a look at the corpse.
Excuse my caution, but I'm bound to verify a bit if I can.'

He shook his head mournfully. 'I reckoned you'd ask for
that, but I haven't got it. It's on my chain on the dressing-table.
I had to leave it behind, for I couldn't leave any clues to breed
suspicions. The gentry who are after me are pretty bright-eyed
citizens. You'll have to take me on trust for the night, and
to-morrow you'll get proof of the corpse business right enough.'

I thought for an instant or two. 'Right. I'll trust you for the night. I'll lock you into this room and keep the key. Just one word, Mr Scudder. I believe you're straight, but if so be you are not I should warn you that I'm a handy man with a gun.'

'Sure,' he said, jumping up with some briskness. 'I haven't the privilege of your name, sir, but let me tell you that you're a white man. I'll thank you to lend me a razor.'

I took him into my bedroom and turned him loose. In half an hour's time a figure came out that I scarcely recognised. Only his gimlety hungry eyes were the same. He was shaved clean, his hair was parted in the middle, and he had cut his eyebrows. Further, he carried himself as if he had been drilled, and was the very model, even to the brown complexion, of some British officer who had had a long spell in India. He had a monocle, too, which he stuck in his eye, and every trace of the American had gone out of his speech.

'My hat! Mr Scudder —' I stammered.

'Not Mr Scudder,' he corrected; 'Captain Theophilus Digby, of the 40th Gurkhas, presently home on leave. I'll thank you to remember that, sir.'

I made him up a bed in my smoking room and sought my own couch, more cheerful than I had been for the past month. Things did happen occasionally, even in this God-forgotten metropolis.

I woke next morning to hear my man, Paddock, making the deuce of a row at the smoking-room door. Paddock was a fellow I had done a good turn to out on the Selakwi,[10] and I had inspanned[11] him as my servant as soon as I got to England. He had about as much gift of the gab as a hippopotamus, and was not a great hand at valeting, but I knew I could count on his loyalty.

'Stop that row, Paddock,' I said. 'There's a friend of mine, Captain – Captain' (I couldn't remember the name) 'dossing down in there. Get breakfast for two and then come and speak to me.'

I told Paddock a fine story about how my friend was a great swell, with his nerves pretty bad from overwork, who wanted absolute rest and stillness. Nobody had got to know he was here, or he would be besieged by communications from the India Office and the Prime Minister and his cure would be ruined. I am bound to say Scudder played up splendidly when he came to breakfast. He fixed Paddock with his eyeglass, just like a British officer, asked him about the Boer War, and slung out at me a lot of stuff about imaginary pals. Paddock couldn't learn to call me 'sir,' but he 'sirred' Scudder as if his life depended on it.

I left him with the newspaper and a box of cigars, and went down to the City till luncheon. When I got back the liftman had an important face.

'Nawsty business 'ere this morning, sir. Gent in No. 15 been and shot 'isself. They've just took 'im to the mortiary. The police are up there now.'

I ascended to No. 15, and found a couple of bobbies and an inspector busy making an examination. I asked a few idiotic questions, and they soon kicked me out. Then I found the man that had valeted Scudder, and pumped him, but I could see he suspected nothing. He was a whining fellow with a churchyard face, and half-a-crown went far to console him.

I attended the inquest next day. A partner of some publishing firm gave evidence that the deceased had brought him wood-pulp propositions, and had been, he believed, an agent of an American business. The jury found it a case of suicide while of unsound mind, and the few effects were handed over to the American Consul to deal with. I gave Scudder a full account of the affair, and it interested him greatly. He said he wished he could have attended the inquest, for he reckoned it would be about as spicy as to read one's own obituary notice.

The first two days he stayed with me in that back room he was very peaceful. He read and smoked a bit, and made a heap of jottings in a note-book, and every night we had a game of chess, at which he beat me hollow. I think he was nursing his nerves back to health, for he had had a pretty trying time. But on the third day I could see he was beginning to get restless. He fixed up a list of the days till June 15th, and ticked each off with a red pencil, making remarks in shorthand against them. I would find him sunk in a brown study, with his sharp eyes abstracted, and after those spells of meditation he was apt to be very despondent.

Then I could see that he began to get edgy again. He listened for little noises, and was always asking me if Paddock could be trusted. Once or twice he got very peevish, and apologised for it. I didn't blame him. I made every allowance, for he had taken on a fairly stiff job.

It was not the safety of his own skin that troubled him, but the success of the scheme he had planned. That little man was clean grit all through, without a soft spot in him. One night he was very solemn.

'Say, Hannay,' he said, 'I judge I should let you a bit deeper into this business. I should hate to go out without leaving somebody else to put up a fight.' And he began to tell me in detail what I had only heard from him vaguely.

I did not give him very close attention. The fact is, I was more interested in his own adventures than in his high politics. I reckoned that Karolides and his affairs were not my business, leaving all that to him. So a lot that he said slipped clean out of my memory. I remember that he was very clear that the danger to Karolides would not begin till he had got to London, and would come from the very highest quarters, where there would be no thought of suspicion. He mentioned the name of a woman – Julia Czechenyi – as having something to do with the danger. She would be the decoy, I gathered, to get Karolides out of the care of his guards. He talked, too, about a Black Stone and a man that lisped in his speech, and he described very particularly somebody that he never referred to without a shudder – an old man with a young voice who could hood his eyes like a hawk.

He spoke a good deal about death, too. He was mortally anxious about winning through with his job, but he didn't care a rush for his life.

'I reckon it's like going to sleep when you are pretty well tired out, and waking to find a summer day with the scent of hay coming in at the window. I used to thank God for such mornings way back in the Blue-Grass country,[12] and I guess I'll thank Him when I wake up on the other side of Jordan.'

Next day he was much more cheerful, and read the life of

Stonewall Jackson much of the time. I went out to dinner with a mining engineer I had got to see on business, and came back about half past ten in time for our game of chess before turning in.

I had a cigar in my mouth, I remember as I pushed open the smoking-room door. The lights were not lit, which struck me as odd. I wondered if Scudder had turned in already.

I snapped the switch, but there was nobody there. Then I saw something in the far corner which made me drop my cigar and fall into a cold sweat.

My guest was lying sprawled on his back. There was a long knife through his heart which skewered him to the floor.

CHAPTER II

THE MILKMAN SETS OUT
ON HIS TRAVELS

I sat down in an arm-chair and felt very sick. That lasted for maybe five minutes, and was succeeded by a fit of the horrors. The poor staring white face on the floor was more than I could bear, and I managed to get a table-cloth and cover it. Then I staggered to a cupboard, found the brandy and swallowed several mouthfuls. I had seen men die violently before; indeed I had killed a few myself in the Matabele War;[1] but this cold-blooded indoor business was different. Still I managed to pull myself together. I looked at my watch, and saw that it was half-past ten.

An idea seized me, and I went over the flat with a small-tooth comb. There was nobody there, nor any trace of anybody, but I shuttered and bolted all the windows and put the chain on the door.

By this time my wits were coming back to me, and I could think again. It took me about an hour to figure the thing out, and I did not hurry, for, unless the murderer came back, I had till about six o'clock in the morning for my cogitations.

I was in the soup – that was pretty clear. Any shadow of a doubt I might have had about the truth of Scudder's tale was now gone. The proof of it was lying under the table-cloth. The men who knew that he knew what he knew had found him, and had taken the best way to make certain of his silence. Yes; but he had been in my rooms four days, and his enemies must have reckoned that he had confided in me. So I would be the next to go. It might be that very night, or next day, or the day after, but my number was up all right.

Then suddenly I thought of another probability. Supposing I

went out now and called in the police, or went to bed and let Paddock find the body and call them in the morning. What kind of a story was I to tell about Scudder? I had lied to Paddock about him, and the whole thing looked desperately fishy. If I made a clean breast of it and told the police everything he had told me, they would simply laugh at me. The odds were a thousand to one that I would be charged with the murder, and the circumstantial evidence was strong enough to hang me. Few people knew me in England; I had no real pal who could come forward and swear to my character. Perhaps that was what those secret enemies were playing for. They were clever enough for anything, and an English prison was as good a way of getting rid of me till after June 15th as a knife in my chest.

Besides, if I told the whole story, and by any miracle was believed, I would be playing their game. Karolides would stay at home, which was what they wanted. Somehow or other the sight of Scudder's dead face had made me a passionate believer in his scheme. He was gone, but he had taken me into his confidence, and I was pretty well bound to carry on his work.

You may think this ridiculous for a man in danger of his life, but that was the way I looked at it. I am an ordinary sort of fellow, not braver than other people, but I hate to see a good man downed, and that long knife would not be the end of Scudder if I could play the game in his place.

It took me an hour or two to think this out, and by that time I had come to a decision. I must vanish somehow, and keep vanished till the end of the second week in June. Then I must somehow find a way to get in touch with the Government people and tell them what Scudder had told me. I wished to heaven he had told me more, and that I had listened more carefully to the little he had told me. I knew nothing but the barest facts. There was a big risk that, even if I weathered the other dangers, I would not be believed in the end. I must take my chance of that, and hope that something might happen which would confirm my tale in the eyes of the Government.

My first job was to keep going for the next three weeks. It was now the 24th day of May, and that meant twenty days of hiding before I could venture to approach the powers that be.

I reckoned that two sets of people would be looking for me – Scudder's enemies to put me out of existence, and the police, who would want me for Scudder's murder. It was going to be a giddy hunt, and it was queer how the prospect comforted me. I had been slack so long that almost any chance of activity was welcome. When I had to sit alone with that corpse and wait on Fortune I was no better than a crushed worm, but if my neck's safety was to hang on my own wits I was prepared to be cheerful about it.

My next thought was whether Scudder had any papers about him to give me a better clue to the business. I drew back the table-cloth and searched his pockets, for I had no longer any shrinking from the body. The face was wonderfully calm for a man who had been struck down in a moment. There was nothing in the breast-pocket, and only a few loose coins and a cigar-holder in the waistcoat. The trousers held a little penknife and some silver, and the side-pocket of his jacket contained an old crocodile-skin cigar-case. There was no sign of the little black book in which I had seen him making notes. That had no doubt been taken by his murderer.

But as I looked up from my task I saw that some drawers had been pulled out in the writing-table. Scudder would never have left them in that state, for he was the tidiest of mortals. Some one must have been searching for something – perhaps for the pocket-book.

I went round the flat and found that everything had been ransacked – the inside of books, drawers, cupboards, boxes, even the pockets of the clothes in my wardrobe, and the side-board in the dining-room. There was no trace of the book. Most likely the enemy had found it, but they had not found it on Scudder's body.

Then I got out an atlas and looked at a big map of the British Isles. My notion was to get off to some wild district, where my veldcraft would be of some use to me, for I would be like a trapped rat in a city. I considered that Scotland would be best, for my people were Scotch and I could pass anywhere as an ordinary Scotsman. I had half an idea at first to be a German tourist, for my father had had German partners, and I had been

brought up to speak the tongue pretty fluently, not to mention
having put in three years prospecting for copper in German
Damaraland.[2] But I calculated that it would be less conspicuous
to be a Scot, and less in a line with what the police might know
of my past. I fixed on Galloway[3] as the best place to go to. It
was the nearest wild part of Scotland, so far as I could figure it
out, and from the look of the map was not over thick with
population.

A search in Bradshaw[4] informed me that a train left St Pancras
at 7.10, which would land me at any Galloway station in the
late afternoon. That was well enough, but a more important
matter was how I was to make my way to St Pancras, for I was
pretty certain that Scudder's friends would be watching outside.
This puzzled me for a bit; then I had an inspiration, on which I
went to bed and slept for two troubled hours.

I got up at four and opened my bedroom shutters. The faint
light of a fine summer morning was flooding the skies, and the
sparrows had begun to chatter. I had a great revulsion of feeling,
and felt a God-forgotten fool. My inclination was to let things
slide, and trust to the British police taking a reasonable view of
my case. But as I reviewed the situation I could find no arguments
to bring against my decision of the previous night, so with a wry
mouth I resolved to go on with my plan. I was not feeling in any
particular funk; only disinclined to go looking for trouble, if
you understand me.

I hunted out a well-used tweed suit, a pair of strong nailed
boots, and a flannel shirt with a collar. Into my pockets I
stuffed a spare shirt, a cloth cap, some handkerchiefs, and a
tooth-brush. I had drawn a good sum in gold from the bank
two days before, in case Scudder should want money, and I took
fifty pounds of it in sovereigns in a belt which I had brought
back from Rhodesia. That was about all I wanted. Then I had a
bath, and cut my moustache, which was long and drooping,
into a short stubbly fringe.

Now came the next step. Paddock used to arrive punctually
at 7.30 and let himself in with a latch-key. But about twenty
minutes to seven, as I knew from bitter experience, the milkman
turned up with a great clatter of cans, and deposited my share

outside my door. I had seen that milkman sometimes when I had gone out for an early ride. He was a young man about my own height, with an ill-nourished moustache, and he wore a white overall. On him I staked all my chances.

I went into the darkened smoking-room where the rays of morning light were beginning to creep through the shutters. There I breakfasted off a whisky-and-soda and some biscuits from the cupboard. By this time it was getting on for six o'clock. I put a pipe in my pocket and filled my pouch from the tobacco jar on the table by the fireplace.

As I poked into the tobacco my fingers touched something hard, and I drew out Scudder's little black pocket-book . . .

That seemed to me a good omen. I lifted the cloth from the body and was amazed at the peace and dignity of the dead face. 'Good-bye, old chap,' I said; 'I am going to do my best for you. Wish me well, wherever you are.'

Then I hung about in the hall waiting for the milkman. That was the worst part of the business, for I was fairly choking to get out of doors. Six-thirty passed, then six-forty, but still he did not come. The fool had chosen this day of all days to be late.

At one minute after the quarter to seven I heard the rattle of the cans outside. I opened the front door, and there was my man, singling out my cans from a bunch he carried and whistling through his teeth. He jumped a bit at the sight of me.

'Come in here a moment,' I said. 'I want a word with you.' And I led him into the dining-room.

'I reckon you're a bit of a sportsman,' I said, 'and I want you to do me a service. Lend me your cap and overall for ten minutes, and here's a sovereign for you.'

His eyes opened at the sight of the gold, and he grinned broadly. 'Wot's the gyme?' he asked.

'A bet,' I said. 'I haven't time to explain, but to win it I've got to be a milkman for the next ten minutes. All you've got to do is to stay here till I come back. You'll be a bit late, but nobody will complain, and you'll have that quid for yourself.'

'Right-O!' he said cheerily. 'I ain't the man to spoil a bit of sport. 'Ere's the rig, guv'nor.'

I stuck on his flat blue hat and his white overall, picked up the cans, banged my door, and went whistling downstairs. The porter at the foot told me to shut my jaw, which sounded as if my make-up was adequate.

At first I thought there was nobody in the street. Then I caught sight of a policeman a hundred yards down, and a loafer shuffling past on the other side. Some impulse made me raise my eyes to the house opposite, and there at a first-floor window was a face. As the loafer passed he looked up and I fancied a signal was exchanged.

I crossed the street, whistling gaily and imitating the jaunty swing of the milkman. Then I took the first side street, and went up a left-hand turning which led past a bit of vacant ground. There was no one in the little street, so I dropped the milk-cans inside the hoarding and sent the hat and overall after them. I had only just put on my cloth cap when a postman came round the corner. I gave him good-morning and he answered me unsuspiciously. At the moment the clock of a neighbouring church struck the hour of seven.

There was not a second to spare. As soon as I got to Euston Road I took to my heels and ran. The clock at Euston Station showed five minutes past the hour. At St Pancras I had no time to take a ticket, let alone that I had not settled upon my destination. A porter told me the platform, and as I entered it I saw the train already in motion. Two station officials blocked the way, but I dodged them and clambered into the last carriage.

Three minutes later, as we were roaring through the northern tunnels, an irate guard interviewed me. He wrote out for me a ticket to Newton-Stewart, a name which had suddenly come back to my memory, and he conducted me from the first-class compartment where I had ensconced myself to a third-class smoker, occupied by a sailor and a stout woman with a child. He went off grumbling, and as I mopped my brow I observed to my companions in my broadest Scots that it was a sore job catching trains. I had already entered upon my part.

'The impidence o' that gyaird!' said the lady bitterly. 'He needit a Scotch tongue to pit him in his place. He was complainin' o' this wean no haein' a ticket and her no fower till

August twalmonth, and he was objectin' to this gentleman spittin'.'

The sailor morosely agreed, and I started my new life in an atmosphere of protest against authority. I reminded myself that a week ago I had been finding the world dull.

CHAPTER III
THE ADVENTURE OF THE LITERARY INNKEEPER

I had a solemn time travelling north that day. It was fine May weather, with the hawthorn flowering on every hedge, and I asked myself why, when I was still a free man, I had stayed on in London and not got the good of this heavenly country. I didn't dare face the restaurant car, but I got a luncheon-basket at Leeds and shared it with the fat woman. Also I got the morning's papers, with news about starters for the Derby and the beginning of the cricket season, and some paragraphs about how Balkan affairs were settling down and a British squadron was going to Kiel.[1]

When I had done with them I got out Scudder's little black pocket-book and studied it. It was pretty well filled with jottings, chiefly figures, though now and then a name was printed in. For example, I found the words 'Hofgaard,' 'Luneville,' and 'Avocado' pretty often, and especially the word 'Pavia.'

Now I was certain that Scudder never did anything without a reason, and I was pretty sure that there was a cypher in all this. That is a subject which has always interested me, and I did a bit at it myself once as intelligence-officer at Delagoa Bay[2] during the Boer War. I have a head for things like chess and puzzles, and I used to reckon myself pretty good at finding out cyphers. This one looked like the numerical kind where sets of figures correspond to the letters of the alphabet, but any fairly shrewd man can find the clue to that sort after an hour or two's work, and I didn't think Scudder would have been content with anything so easy. So I fastened on the printed words, for you can make a pretty good numerical cypher if you have a key word which gives you the sequence of the letters.

I tried for hours, but none of the words answered. Then I fell asleep and woke at Dumfries just in time to bundle out and get into the slow Galloway train. There was a man on the platform whose looks I didn't like, but he never glanced at me, and when I caught sight of myself in the mirror of an automatic machine I didn't wonder. With my brown face, my old tweeds, and my slouch, I was the very model of one of the hill farmers who were crowding into the third-class carriages.

I travelled with half a dozen in an atmosphere of shag[3] and clay pipes. They had come from the weekly market, and their mouths were full of prices. I heard accounts of how the lambing had gone up the Cairn and the Deuch and a dozen other mysterious waters. Above half the men had lunched heavily and were highly flavoured with whisky, but they took no notice of me. We rumbled slowly into a land of little wooded glens and then to a great wide moorland place, gleaming with lochs, with high blue hills showing northwards.

About five o'clock the carriage had emptied, and I was left alone as I had hoped. I got out at the next station, a little place whose name I scarcely noted, set right in the heart of a bog. It reminded me of one of those forgotten little stations in the Karroo.[4] An old station-master was digging in his garden, and with his spade over his shoulder sauntered to the train, took charge of a parcel, and went back to his potatoes. A child of ten received my ticket, and I emerged on a white road that straggled over the brown moor.

It was a gorgeous spring evening, with every hill showing as clear as a cut amethyst. The air had the queer, rooty smell of bogs, but it was as fresh as mid-ocean, and it had the strangest effect on my spirits. I actually felt light-hearted. I might have been a boy out for a spring holiday tramp, instead of a man of thirty-seven very much wanted by the police. I felt just as I used to feel when I was starting for a big trek on a frosty morning on the high veld. If you believe me, I swung along that road whistling. There was no plan of campaign in my head, only just to go on and on in this blessed, honest-smelling hill country, for every mile put me in better humour with myself.

In a roadside planting I cut a walking-stick of hazel, and

presently struck off the highway up a bypath which followed the glen of a brawling stream. I reckoned that I was still far ahead of any pursuit, and for that night might please myself. It was some hours since I had tasted food, and I was getting very hungry when I came to a herd's cottage set in a nook beside a waterfall. A brown-faced woman was standing by the door, and greeted me with the kindly shyness of moorland places. When I asked for a night's lodging she said I was welcome to the 'bed in the loft,' and very soon she set before me a hearty meal of ham and eggs, scones, and thick sweet milk.

At the darkening her man came in from the hills, a lean giant, who in one step covered as much ground as three paces of ordinary mortals. They asked no questions, for they had the perfect breeding of all dwellers in the wilds, but I could see they set me down as a kind of dealer, and I took some trouble to confirm their view. I spoke a lot about cattle, of which my host knew little, and I picked up from him a good deal about the local Galloway markets, which I tucked away in my memory for future use. At ten I was nodding in my chair, and the 'bed in the loft' received a weary man who never opened his eyes till five o'clock set the little homestead agoing once more.

They refused any payment, and by six I had breakfasted and was striding southwards again. My notion was to return to the railway line a station or two farther on than the place where I had alighted yesterday and to double back. I reckoned that that was the safest way, for the police would naturally assume that I was always making farther from London in the direction of some western port. I thought I had still a good bit of a start, for, as I reasoned, it would take some hours to fix the blame on me, and several more to identify the fellow who got on board the train at St Pancras.

It was the same jolly, clear spring weather, and I simply could not contrive to feel careworn. Indeed I was in better spirits than I had been for months. Over a long ridge of moorland I took my road, skirting the side of a high hill which the herd had called Cairnsmore of Fleet. Nesting curlews and plovers were crying everywhere, and the links of green pasture by the streams were dotted with young lambs. All the slackness of the past months was slipping from my bones, and I stepped out like a four-year-old. By-and-by I came to a swell of moorland which dipped to the vale of a little river, and a mile away in the heather I saw the smoke of a train.

The station, when I reached it, proved to be ideal for my purpose. The moor surged up around it and left room only for the single line, the slender siding, a waiting-room, an office, the station-master's cottage, and a tiny yard of gooseberries and sweet-william. There seemed no road to it from anywhere, and to increase the desolation the waves of a tarn[5] lapped on their grey granite beach half a mile away. I waited in the deep heather till I saw the smoke of an east-going train on the horizon. Then I approached the tiny booking-office and took a ticket for Dumfries.

The only occupants of the carriage were an old shepherd and his dog – a wall-eyed brute that I mistrusted. The man was asleep, and on the cushions beside him was that morning's *Scotsman*. Eagerly I seized on it, for I fancied it would tell me something.

There were two columns about the Portland Place Murder, as it was called. My man Paddock had given the alarm and had the milkman arrested. Poor devil, it looked as if the latter had earned his sovereign hardly; but for me he had been cheap at the price, for he seemed to have occupied the police the better part of the day. In the latest news I found a further instalment of the story. The milkman had been released, I read, and the true criminal, about whose identity the police were reticent, was believed to have got away from London by one of the northern lines. There was a short note about me as the owner of the flat. I guessed the police had stuck that in, as a clumsy contrivance to persuade me that I was unsuspected.

There was nothing else in the paper, nothing about foreign politics or Karolides, or the things that had interested Scudder. I laid it down, and found that we were approaching the station at which I had got out yesterday. The potato-digging station-master had been gingered up into some activity, for the west-going train was waiting to let us pass, and from it had descended three men who were asking him questions. I supposed that they were the local police, who had been stirred up by Scotland Yard, and had traced me as far as this one-horse siding. Sitting well back in the shadow I watched them carefully. One of them had a book, and took down notes. The old potato-digger seemed to have turned peevish, but the child who had collected my ticket was talking volubly. All the party looked out across the moor where the white road departed. I hoped they were going to take up my tracks there.

As we moved away from that station my companion woke up. He fixed me with a wandering glance, kicked his dog viciously, and inquired where he was. Clearly he was very drunk.

'That's what comes o' bein' a teetotaller,' he observed in bitter regret.

I expressed my surprise that in him I should have met a blue-ribbon[6] stalwart.

'Ay, but I'm a strong teetotaller,' he said pugnaciously. 'I took the pledge last Martinmas, and I havena touched a drop o' whisky sinsyne. No even at Hogmanay, though I was sair temptit.'

He swung his heels up on the seat, and burrowed a frowsy head into the cushions.

'And that's a' I get,' he moaned. 'A heid hetter than hell fire, and twae een lookin' different ways for the Sabbath.'

'What did it?' I asked.

'A drink they ca' brandy. Bein' a teetotaller I keepit off the whisky, but I was nip-nippin' a' day at this brandy, and I doubt I'll no be weel for a fortnicht.' His voice died away into a stutter, and sleep once more laid its heavy hand on him.

My plan had been to get out at some station down the line, but the train suddenly gave me a better chance, for it came to a standstill at the end of a culvert which spanned a brawling porter-coloured river. I looked out and saw that every carriage window was closed and no human figure appeared in the landscape. So I opened the door, and dropped quickly into the tangle of hazels which edged the line.

It would have been all right but for that infernal dog. Under the impression that I was decamping with its master's belongings, it started to bark, and all but got me by the trousers. This woke up the herd, who stood bawling at the carriage door in the belief that I had committed suicide. I crawled through the thicket, reached the edge of the stream, and in cover of the bushes put a hundred yards or so behind me. Then from my shelter I peered back, and saw the guard and several passengers gathered round the open carriage door and staring in my direction. I could not have made a more public departure if I had left with a bugler and a brass band.

Happily the drunken herd provided a diversion. He and his dog, which was attached by a rope to his waist, suddenly cascaded out of the carriage, landed on their heads on the track, and rolled some way down the bank towards the water. In the rescue which followed the dog bit somebody, for I could hear the sound of hard swearing. Presently they had forgotten me, and when after a quarter of a mile's crawl I ventured to look back, the train had started again and was vanishing in the cutting.

I was in a wide semicircle of moorland, with the brown river as radius, and the high hills forming the northern circumference. There was not a sign or sound of a human being, only the plashing water and the interminable crying of curlews. Yet, oddly enough, for the first time I felt the terror of the hunted on me. It was not the police that I thought of, but the other folk, who knew that I knew Scudder's secret and dared not let me live. I was certain that they would pursue me with a keenness and vigilance unknown to the British law, and that once their grip closed on me I should find no mercy.

I looked back, but there was nothing in the landscape. The sun glinted on the metals of the line and the wet stones in the stream, and you could not have found a more peaceful sight in the world. Nevertheless I started to run. Crouching low in the runnels of the bog, I ran till the sweat blinded my eyes. The mood did not leave me till I had reached the rim of mountain and flung myself panting on a ridge high above the young waters of the brown river.

From my vantage-ground I could scan the whole moor right away to the railway line and to the south of it where green fields took the place of heather. I have eyes like a hawk, but I could see nothing moving in the whole countryside. Then I looked east beyond the ridge and saw a new kind of landscape – shallow green valleys with plentiful fir plantations and the faint lines of dust which spoke of highroads. Last of all I looked into the blue May sky, and there I saw that which set my pulses racing . . .

Low down in the south a monoplane was climbing into the heavens. I was as certain as if I had been told that that aeroplane was looking for me, and that it did not belong to the police. For an hour or two I watched it from a pit of heather. It flew low along the hill-tops, and then in narrow circles over the valley up which I had come. Then it seemed to change its mind, rose to a great height, and flew away back to the south.

I did not like this espionage from the air, and I began to think less well of the countryside I had chosen for a refuge. These heather hills were no sort of cover if my enemies were in the sky, and I must find a different kind of sanctuary. I looked with more satisfaction to the green country beyond the ridge, for there I should find woods and stone houses.

About six in the evening I came out of the moorland to a white ribbon of road which wound up the narrow vale of a lowland stream. As I followed it, fields gave place to bent,[7] the glen became a plateau, and presently I had reached a kind of pass where a solitary house smoked in the twilight. The road swung over a bridge, and leaning on the parapet was a young man.

He was smoking a long clay pipe and studying the water with spectacled eyes. In his left hand was a small book with a finger marking the place. Slowly he repeated –

> 'As when a Gryphon through the wilderness
>   With wingéd step, o'er hill and moory dale
>   Pursues the Arimaspian.'[8]

He jumped round as my step rung on the keystone, and I saw a pleasant sunburnt boyish face.

'Good evening to you,' he said gravely. 'It's a fine night for the road.'

The smell of peat smoke and of some savoury roast floated to me from the house.

'Is that place an inn?' I asked.

'At your service,' he said politely. 'I am the landlord, sir, and I hope you will stay the night, for to tell you the truth I have had no company for a week.'

I pulled myself up on the parapet of the bridge and filled my pipe. I began to detect an ally.

'You're young to be an innkeeper,' I said.

'My father died a year ago and left me the business. I live there with my grandmother. It's a slow job for a young man, and it wasn't my choice of profession.'

'Which was?'

He actually blushed. 'I want to write books,' he said.

'And what better chance could you ask?' I cried. 'Man, I've often thought that an innkeeper would make the best story-teller in the world.'

'Not now,' he said eagerly. 'Maybe in the old days when you had pilgrims and ballad-makers and highwaymen and mail-coaches on the road. But not now. Nothing comes here but motor-cars full of fat women, who stop for lunch, and a fisher-man or two in the spring, and the shooting tenants in August. There is not much material to be got out of that. I want to see life, to travel the world, and write things like Kipling and Conrad. But the most I've done yet is to get some verses printed in *Chambers's Journal*.'[9]

I looked at the inn standing golden in the sunset against the brown hills.

'I've knocked a bit about the world, and I wouldn't despise such a hermitage. D'you think that adventure is found only in the tropics or among gentry in red shirts? Maybe you're rubbing shoulders with it at this moment.'

'That's what Kipling says,' he said, his eyes brightening, and he quoted some verse about 'Romance bringing up the 9.15.'

'Here's a true tale for you then,' I cried, 'and a month from now you can make a novel out of it.'

Sitting on the bridge in the soft May gloaming I pitched him a lovely yarn. It was true in essentials, too, though I altered the minor details. I made out that I was a mining magnate from Kimberley, who had had a lot of trouble with I.D.B.[10] and had shown up a gang. They had pursued me across the ocean, and had killed my best friend, and were now on my tracks.

I told the story well, though I say it who shouldn't. I pictured a flight across the Kalahari[11] to German Africa, the crackling, parching days, the wonderful blue-velvet nights. I described an attack on my life on the voyage home, and I made a really horrid affair of the Portland Place murder. 'You're looking for adventure,' I cried; 'well, you've found it here. The devils are after me, and the police are after them. It's a race that I mean to win.'

'By God!' he whispered, drawing his breath in sharply, 'it is all pure Rider Haggard and Conan Doyle.'

'You believe me,' I said gratefully.

'Of course I do,' and he held out his hand. 'I believe everything out of the common. The only thing to distrust is the normal.'

He was very young, but he was the man for my money.

'I think they're off my track for the moment, but I must lie close for a couple of days. Can you take me in?'

He caught my elbow in his eagerness and drew me towards the house. 'You can lie as snug here as if you were in a moss-hole. I'll see that nobody blabs, either. And you'll give me some more material about your adventures?'

As I entered the inn porch I heard from far off the beat of an engine. There silhouetted against the dusky West was my friend, the monoplane.

He gave me a room at the back of the house, with a fine outlook over the plateau, and he made me free of his own study, which was stacked with cheap editions of his favourite authors. I never saw the grandmother, so I guessed she was bed-ridden. An old woman called Margit brought me my meals, and the innkeeper was around me at all hours. I wanted some time to myself, so I invented a job for him. He had a motor bicycle, and I sent him off next morning for the daily paper, which usually arrived with the post in the late afternoon. I told him to keep his eyes skinned, and make note of any strange figures he saw, keeping a special sharp look-out for motors and aeroplanes. Then I sat down in real earnest to Scudder's note-book.

He came back at midday with the *Scotsman*. There was nothing in it, except some further evidence of Paddock and the milkman, and a repetition of yesterday's statement that the murderer had gone North. But there was a long article, reprinted from the *Times*, about Karolides and the state of affairs in the Balkans, though there was no mention of any visit to England. I got rid of the innkeeper for the afternoon, for I was getting very warm in my search for the cypher.

As I told you, it was a numerical cypher, and by an elaborate system of experiments I had pretty well discovered what were the nulls and stops. The trouble was the key word, and when I thought of the odd million words he might have used I felt pretty hopeless. But about three o'clock I had a sudden inspiration.

The name Julia Czechenyi flashed across my memory. Scudder had said it was the key to the Karolides business, and it occurred to me to try it on his cypher.

It worked. The five letters of 'Julia' gave me the position of the vowels. A was J, the tenth letter of the alphabet, and so represented by X in the cypher. E was U = XXI, and so on. 'Czechenyi' gave me the numerals for the principal consonants. I scribbled that scheme on a bit of paper and sat down to read Scudder's pages.

In half an hour I was reading with a whitish face and fingers that drummed on the table.

I glanced out of the window and saw a big touring-car coming up the glen towards the inn. It drew up at the door, and there was the sound of people alighting. There seemed to be two of them, men in aquascutums and tweed caps.

Ten minutes later the innkeeper slipped into the room, his eyes bright with excitement.

'There's two chaps below looking for you,' he whispered. 'They're in the dining-room having whiskys and sodas. They asked about you and said they had hoped to meet you here. Oh! and they described you jolly well, down to your boots and shirt. I told them you had been here last night and had gone off on a motor bicycle this morning, and one of the chaps swore like a navvy.'

I made him tell me what they looked like. One was a dark-eyed thin fellow with bushy eyebrows, the other was always smiling and lisped in his talk. Neither was any kind of foreigner; on this my young friend was positive.

I took a bit of paper and wrote these words in German as if they were part of a letter:–

... 'Black Stone. Scudder had got on to this, but he could not act for a fortnight. I doubt if I can do any good now, especially as Karolides is uncertain about his plans. But if Mr T. advises I will do the best I ...'

I manufactured it rather neatly, so that it looked like a loose page of a private letter.

'Take this down and say it was found in my bedroom, and ask them to return it to me if they overtake me.'

Three minutes later I heard the car begin to move, and peeping from behind the curtain caught sight of the two figures. One was slim, the other was sleek; that was the most I could make of my reconnaissance.

The innkeeper appeared in great excitement. 'Your paper woke them up,' he said gleefully. 'The dark fellow went as white as death and cursed like blazes, and the fat one whistled and looked ugly. They paid for their drinks with half-a-sovereign and wouldn't wait for change.'

'Now I'll tell you what I want you to do,' I said. 'Get on your bicycle and go off to Newton-Stewart to the Chief Constable. Describe the two men, and say you suspect them of having had something to do with the London murder. You can invent reasons. The two will come back, never fear. Not to-night, for they'll follow me forty miles along the road, but first thing to-morrow morning. Tell the police to be here bright and early.'

He set off like a docile child, while I worked at Scudder's notes. When he came back we dined together, and in common decency I had to let him pump me. I gave him a lot of stuff about lion hunts and the Matabele War, thinking all the while what tame businesses these were compared to this I was now engaged in. When he went to bed I sat up and finished Scudder. I smoked in a chair till daylight, for I could not sleep.

About eight next morning I witnessed the arrival of two constables and a sergeant. They put their car in a coach-house under the innkeeper's instructions, and entered the house. Twenty minutes later I saw from my window a second car come across the plateau from the opposite direction. It did not come up to the inn, but stopped two hundred yards off in the shelter of a patch of wood. I noticed that its occupants carefully reversed it before leaving it. A minute or two later I heard their steps on the gravel outside the window.

My plan had been to lie hid in my bedroom, and see what happened. I had a notion that, if I could bring the police and my other more dangerous pursuers together, something might work out of it to my advantage. But now I had a better idea. I scribbled a line of thanks to my host, opened the window, and dropped quietly into a gooseberry bush. Unobserved I crossed the dyke, crawled down the side of a tributary burn,[12] and won the highroad on the far side of the patch of trees. There stood the car, very spick and span in the morning sunlight, but with the dust on her which told of a long journey. I started her, jumped into the chauffeur's seat, and stole gently out on to the plateau.

Almost at once the road dipped so that I lost sight of the inn, but the wind seemed to bring me the sound of angry voices.

CHAPTER IV

THE ADVENTURE OF THE
RADICAL CANDIDATE

You may picture me driving that 40 h.p. car for all she was worth over the crisp moor roads on that shining May morning; glancing back at first over my shoulder, and looking anxiously to the next turning; then driving with a vague eye, just wide enough awake to keep on the highway. For I was thinking desperately of what I had found in Scudder's pocket-book.

The little man had told me a pack of lies. All his yarns about the Balkans and the Jew-Anarchists and the Foreign Office Conference were eyewash, and so was Karolides. And yet not quite, as you shall hear. I had staked everything on my belief in his story, and had been let down; here was his book telling me a different tale, and instead of being once-bit-twice-shy, I believed it absolutely.

Why, I don't know. It rang desperately true, and the first yarn, if you understand me, had been in a queer way true also in spirit. The fifteenth day of June was going to be a day of destiny, a bigger destiny than the killing of a Dago.[1] It was so big that I didn't blame Scudder for keeping me out of the game and wanting to play a lone hand. That, I was pretty clear, was his intention. He had told me something which sounded big enough, but the real thing was so immortally big that he, the man who had found it out, wanted it all for himself. I didn't blame him. It was risks after all that he was chiefly greedy about.

The whole story was in the notes – with gaps, you understand, which he would have filled up from his memory. He stuck down his authorities, too, and had an odd trick of giving them all a numerical value and then striking a balance, which stood for the reliability of each stage in the yarn. The four names he had printed were authorities, and there was a man, Ducrosne, who got five out of a possible five; and another fellow, Ammersfoort, who got three. The bare bones of the tale were all that was in the book – these, and one queer phrase which occurred half a dozen times inside brackets. ('Thirty-nine steps') was the phrase; and at its last time of use it ran – ('Thirty-nine steps, I counted them – high tide 10.17 P.M.'). I could make nothing of that.

The first thing I learned was that it was no question of preventing a war. That was coming, as sure as Christmas: had been arranged, said Scudder, ever since February 1912. Karolides was going to be the occasion. He was booked all right, and was to hand in his checks on June 14th, two weeks and four days from that May morning. I gathered from Scudder's notes that nothing on earth could prevent that. His talk of Epirote guards that would skin their own grandmothers was all billy-O.

The second thing was that this war was going to come as a mighty surprise to Britain. Karolides' death would set the Balkans by the ears, and then Vienna would chip in with an ultimatum. Russia wouldn't like that, and there would be high words. But Berlin would play the peacemaker, and pour oil on the waters, till suddenly she would find a good cause for a quarrel, pick it up, and in five hours let fly at us. That was the idea, and a pretty good one too. Honey and fair speeches, and then a stroke in the dark. While we were talking about the good-will and good intentions of Germany our coast would be silently ringed with mines, and submarines would be waiting for every battleship.

But all this depended upon the third thing, which was due to happen on June 15th. I would never have grasped this if I hadn't once happened to meet a French staff officer, coming back from West Africa, who had told me a lot of things. One was that, in spite of all the nonsense talked in Parliament, there was a real working alliance between France and Britain, and that the two General Staffs met every now and then, and made plans for joint action in case of war.[2] Well, in June a very great swell was coming over from Paris, and he was going to get nothing less than a statement of the disposition of the British Home Fleet on mobilisation. At least I gathered it was something like that; anyhow, it was something uncommonly important.

But on the 15th day of June there were to be others in London – others, at whom I could only guess. Scudder was content to call them collectively the 'Black Stone.' They represented not our Allies, but our deadly foes; and the information, destined for France, was to be diverted to their pockets. And it was to be used, remember – used a week or two later, with great guns and swift torpedoes, suddenly in the darkness of a summer night.

This was the story I had been deciphering in a back-room of a country inn, overlooking a cabbage garden. This was the story that hummed in my brain as I swung in the big touring-car from glen to glen.

My first impulse had been to write a letter to the Prime Minister, but a little reflection convinced me that that would be useless. Who would believe my tale? I must show a sign, some token in proof, and Heaven knew what that could be. Above all, I must keep going myself, ready to act when things got riper, and that was going to be no light job with the police of the British Isles in full cry after me and the watchers of the Black Stone running silently and swiftly on my trail.

I had no very clear purpose in my journey, but I steered east by the sun, for I remembered from the map that if I went north I would come into a region of coalpits and industrial towns. Presently I was down from the moorlands and traversing the broad haugh³ of a river. For miles I ran alongside a park wall, and in a break of the trees I saw a great castle. I swung through little old thatched villages, and over peaceful lowland streams, and past gardens blazing with hawthorn and yellow laburnum. The land was so deep in peace that I could scarcely believe that somewhere behind me were those who sought my life; ay, and that in a month's time, unless I had the almightiest of luck, these round country faces would be pinched and staring, and men would be lying dead in English fields.

About midday I entered a long straggling village, and had a mind to stop and eat. Half-way down was the Post Office, and on the steps of it stood the post-mistress and a policeman hard at work conning a telegram. When they saw me they wakened up, and the policeman advanced with raised hand, and cried on me to stop.

I nearly was fool enough to obey. Then it flashed upon me that the wire had to do with me; that my friends at the inn had come to an understanding, and were united in desiring to see more of me, and that it had been easy enough for them to wire the description of me and the car to thirty villages through which I might pass. I released the brakes just in time. As it was, the policeman made a claw at the hood, and only dropped off when he got my left in his eye.

I saw that main roads were no place for me, and turned into the byways. It wasn't an easy job without a map, for there was the risk of getting on to a farm road and ending in a duck-pond or a stable-yard, and I couldn't afford that kind of delay. I began to see what an ass I had been to steal the car. The big green brute would be the safest kind of clue to me over the breadth of Scotland. If I left it and took to my feet, it would be discovered in an hour or two and I would get no start in the race.

The immediate thing to do was to get to the loneliest roads. These I soon found when I struck up a tributary of the big river, and got into a glen with steep hills all about me, and a corkscrew road at the end which climbed over a pass. Here I met nobody, but it was taking me too far north, so I slewed east along a bad track and finally struck a big double-line railway. Away below me I saw another broadish valley, and it occurred to me that if I crossed it I might find some remote inn to pass the night. The evening was now drawing in, and I was furiously hungry, for I had eaten nothing since breakfast except a couple of buns I had bought from a baker's cart.

Just then I heard a noise in the sky, and lo and behold there was that infernal aeroplane, flying low, about a dozen miles to the south and rapidly coming towards me.

I had the sense to remember that on a bare moor I was at the aeroplane's mercy, and that my only chance was to get to the leafy cover of the valley. Down the hill I went like blue lightning, screwing my head round, whenever I dared, to watch that damned flying machine. Soon I was on a road between hedges, and dipping to the deep-cut glen of a stream. Then came a bit of thick wood where I slackened speed.

Suddenly on my left I heard the hoot of another car, and realised to my horror that I was almost up on a couple of gate-posts through which a private road debouched on the highway. My horn gave an agonised roar, but it was too late. I clapped on my brakes, but my impetus was too great, and there before me a car was sliding athwart my course. In a second there would have been the deuce of a wreck. I did the only thing possible, and ran slap into the hedge on the right, trusting to find something soft beyond.

But there I was mistaken. My car slithered through the hedge like butter, and then gave a sickening plunge forward. I saw what was coming, leapt on the seat and would have jumped out. But a branch of hawthorn got me in the chest, lifted me up and held me, while a ton or two of expensive metal slipped below me, bucked and pitched, and then dropped with an almighty smash fifty feet to the bed of the stream.

Slowly that thorn let me go. I subsided first on the hedge, and then very gently on a bower of nettles. As I scrambled to my feet a hand took me by the arm, and a sympathetic and badly scared voice asked me if I were hurt.

I found myself looking at a tall young man in goggles and a leather ulster,[4] who kept on blessing his soul and whinnying apologies. For myself, once I got my wind back, I was rather glad than otherwise. This was one way of getting rid of the car.

'My blame, sir,' I answered him. 'It's lucky that I did not add homicide to my follies. That's the end of my Scotch motor tour, but it might have been the end of my life.'

He plucked out a watch and studied it. 'You're the right sort of fellow,' he said. 'I can spare a quarter of an hour, and my house is two minutes off. I'll see you clothed and fed and snug in bed. Where's your kit, by the way? Is it in the burn along with the car?'

'It's in my pocket,' I said, brandishing a tooth-brush. 'I'm a colonial and travel light.'

'A colonial,' he cried. 'By Gad, you're the very man I've been praying for. Are you by any blessed chance a Free Trader?'[5]

'I am,' said I, without the foggiest notion of what he meant.

He patted my shoulder and hurried me into his car. Three minutes later we drew up before a comfortable-looking shooting-box set among pine-trees, and he ushered me indoors. He took me first to a bedroom and flung half a dozen of his suits before me, for my own had been pretty well reduced to rags. I selected a loose blue serge, which differed most conspicuously from my former garments, and borrowed a linen collar. Then he haled me to the dining-room, where the remnants of a meal stood on the table, and announced that I had just five minutes to feed. 'You can take a snack in your pocket, and we'll have supper when we get back. I've got to be at the Masonic Hall at eight o'clock, or my agent will comb my hair.'

I had a cup of coffee and some cold ham, while he yarned away on the hearth-rug.

'You find me in the deuce of a mess, Mr—; by-the-by, you haven't told me your name. Twisdon? Any relation of old Tommy Twisdon of the Sixtieth?[6] No? Well, you see I'm Liberal Candidate for this part of the world, and I had a meeting on to-night at Brattleburn – that's my chief town, and an infernal Tory stronghold. I had got the Colonial ex-Premier fellow, Crumpleton, coming to speak for me to-night, and had the thing tremendously billed and the whole place ground-baited. This afternoon I had a wire from the ruffian saying he had got influenza at Blackpool, and here am I left to do the whole thing myself. I had meant to speak for ten minutes and must now go on for forty, and, though I've been racking my brains for three hours to think of something, I simply cannot last the course. Now you've got to be a good chap and help me. You're a Free Trader and can tell our people what a wash-out Protection[7] is in the Colonies. All you fellows have the gift of the gab – I wish to heaven I had it. I'll be for evermore in your debt.'

I had very few notions about Free Trade one way or the other, but I saw no other chance to get what I wanted. My young gentleman was far too absorbed in his own difficulties to think how odd it was to ask a stranger who had just missed death by an ace and had lost a 1000-guinea[8] car to address a meeting for him on the spur of the moment. But my necessities did not allow me to contemplate oddnesses or to pick and choose my supports.

'All right,' I said. 'I'm not much good as a speaker, but I'll tell them a bit about Australia.'

At my words the cares of the ages slipped from his shoulders, and he was rapturous in his thanks. He lent me a big driving coat – and never troubled to ask why I had started on a motor tour without possessing an ulster – and, as we slipped down the dusty roads, poured into my ears the simple facts of his history. He was an orphan, and his uncle had brought him up – I've forgotten the uncle's name, but he was in the Cabinet, and you can read his speeches in the papers. He had gone round the world after leaving Cambridge, and then, being short of a job, his uncle had advised politics. I gathered that he had no preference in parties. 'Good chaps in both,' he said cheerfully, 'and plenty of blighters, too. I'm Liberal, because my family have always been Whigs.' But if he was lukewarm politically he had strong views on other things. He found out I knew a bit about horses, and jawed away about the Derby entries; and he was full of plans for improving his shooting. Altogether, a very clean, decent, callow young man.

As we passed through a little town two policemen signalled us to stop, and flashed their lanterns on us. 'Beg pardon, Sir Harry,' said one. 'We've got instructions to look out for a cawr, and the description's no unlike yours.'

'Right-O,' said my host, while I thanked Providence for the devious ways I had been brought to safety. After that he spoke no more, for his mind began to labour heavily with his coming speech. His lips kept muttering, his eye wandered, and I began to prepare myself for a second catastrophe. I tried to think of something to say myself, but my mind was dry as a stone. The next thing I knew we had drawn up outside a door in a street, and were being welcomed by some noisy gentlemen with rosettes.

The hall had about five hundred in it, women mostly, a lot of bald heads, and a dozen or two young men. The chairman, a weaselly minister with a reddish nose, lamented Crumpleton's absence, soliloquised on his influenza, and gave me a certificate as a 'trusted leader of Australian thought.' There were two policemen at the door, and I hoped they took note of that testimonial. Then Sir Harry started.

I never heard anything like it. He didn't begin to know how to talk. He had about a bushel of notes from which he read, and when he let go of them he fell into one prolonged stutter. Every now and then he remembered a phrase he had learned by heart, straightened his back, and gave it off like Henry Irving,[9] and the next moment he was bent double and crooning over his papers. It was the most appalling rot, too. He talked about the 'German menace,' and said it was all a Tory invention to cheat the poor of their rights and keep back the great flood of social reform, but that 'organised labour' realised this and laughed the Tories to scorn. He was all for reducing our Navy as a proof of our good faith, and then sending Germany an ultimatum telling her to do the same or we would knock her into a cocked hat. He said that, but for the Tories, Germany and Britain would be fellow-workers in peace and reform. I thought of the little black book in my pocket! A giddy lot Scudder's friends cared for peace and reform.

Yet in a queer way I liked the speech. You could see the niceness of the chap shining out behind the muck with which he had been spoon-fed. Also it took a load off my mind. I mightn't be much of an orator, but I was a thousand per cent better than Sir Harry.

I didn't get on so badly when it came to my turn. I simply told them all I could remember about Australia, praying there should be no Australian there – all about its labour party and emigration and universal service. I doubt if I remembered to mention Free Trade, but I said there were no Tories in Australia, only Labour and Liberals. That fetched a cheer, and I woke them up a bit when I started in to tell them the kind of glorious business I thought could be made out of the Empire if we really put our backs into it.

Altogether I fancy I was rather a success. The minister didn't like me, though, and when he proposed a vote of thanks, spoke of Sir Harry's speech as 'statesmanlike' and mine as having 'the eloquence of an emigration agent.'

When we were in the car again my host was in wild spirits at having got his job over. 'A ripping speech, Twisdon,' he said. 'Now, you're coming home with me. I'm all alone, and if you'll stop a day or two I'll show you some very decent fishing.'

We had a hot supper – and I wanted it pretty badly – and then drank grog in a big cheery smoking-room with a crackling wood fire. I thought the time had come for me to put my cards on the table. I saw by this man's eye that he was the kind you can trust.

'Listen, Sir Harry,' I said. 'I've something pretty important to say to you. You're a good fellow, and I'm going to be frank. Where on earth did you get that poisonous rubbish you talked to-night?'

His face fell. 'Was it as bad as that?' he asked ruefully. 'It did sound rather thin. I got most of it out of the *Progressive Magazine* and pamphlets that agent chap of mine keeps sending me. But you surely don't think Germany would ever go to war with us?'

'Ask that question in six weeks and it won't need an answer,' I said. 'If you'll give me your attention for half an hour I am going to tell you a story.'

I can see yet that bright room with the deers' heads and the old prints on the walls, Sir Harry standing restlessly on the stone curb of the hearth, and myself lying back in an arm-chair, speaking. I seemed to be another person, standing aside and listening to my own voice, and judging carefully the reliability of my tale. It was the first time I had ever told any one the exact truth, so far as I understood it, and it did me no end of good, for it straightened out the thing in my own mind. I blinked no detail. He heard all about Scudder, and the milkman, and the note-book, and my doings in Galloway. Presently he got very excited and walked up and down the hearth-rug.

'So you see,' I concluded, 'you have got here in your house the man that is wanted for the Portland Place murder. Your duty is to send your car for the police and give me up. I don't think I'll get very far. There'll be an accident, and I'll have a knife in my ribs an hour or so after arrest. Nevertheless it's your duty, as a law-abiding citizen. Perhaps in a month's time you'll be sorry, but you have no cause to think of that.'

He was looking at me with bright steady eyes. 'What was your job in Rhodesia, Mr Hannay?' he asked.

'Mining engineer,' I said. 'I've made my pile cleanly and I've had a good time in the making of it.'

'Not a profession that weakens the nerves, is it?'

I laughed. 'Oh, as to that, my nerves are good enough.' I took down a hunting-knife from a stand on the wall, and did the old Mashona[10] trick of tossing it and catching it in my lips. That wants a pretty steady heart.

He watched me with a smile. 'I don't want proofs. I may be an ass on the platform, but I can size up a man. You're no murderer and you're no fool, and I believe you are speaking the truth. I'm going to back you up. Now, what can I do?'

'First, I want you to write a letter to your uncle. I've got to get in touch with the Government people sometime before the 15th of June.'

He pulled his moustache. 'That won't help you. This is Foreign Office business, and my uncle would have nothing to do with it. Besides, you'd never convince him. No, I'll go one better. I'll write to the Permanent Secretary at the Foreign Office. He's my godfather, and one of the best going. What do you want?'

He sat down at a table and wrote to my dictation. The gist of it was that if a man called Twisdon (I thought I had better stick to that name) turned up before June 15th he was to entreat him kindly. He said Twisdon would prove his *bona fides*[11] by passing the word 'Black Stone' and whistling 'Annie Laurie.'

'Good,' said Sir Harry. 'That's the proper style. By the way, you'll find my godfather – his name's Sir Walter Bullivant – down at his country cottage for Whitsuntide. It's close to Artinswell on the Kennet.[12] That's done. Now, what's the next thing?'

'You're about my height. Lend me the oldest tweed suit you've got. Anything will do, so long as the colour is the opposite of the clothes I destroyed this afternoon. Then show me a map of the neighbourhood and explain to me the lie of the land. Lastly, if the police come seeking me, just show them the car in the glen. If the other lot turn up, tell them I caught the south express after your meeting.'

He did, or promised to do, all these things. I shaved off the remnants of my moustache, and got inside an ancient suit of what I believe is called heather mixture. The map gave me some notion of my whereabouts, and told me the two things I wanted to know – where the main railway to the south could be joined and what were the wildest districts near at hand.

At two o'clock he wakened me from my slumbers in the smoking-room arm-chair, and led me blinking into the dark starry night. An old bicycle was found in a tool-shed and handed over to me.

'First turn to the right up by the long fir-wood,' he enjoined. 'By daybreak you'll be well into the hills. Then I should pitch the machine into a bog and take to the moors on foot. You can put in a week among the shepherds, and be as safe as if you were in New Guinea.'

I pedalled diligently up steep roads of hill gravel till the skies grew pale with morning. As the mists cleared before the sun, I found myself in a wide green world with glens falling on every side and a far-away blue horizon. Here, at any rate, I could get early news of my enemies.

CHAPTER V

THE ADVENTURE OF THE SPECTACLED ROADMAN

I sat down on the very crest of the pass and took stock of my position.

Behind me was the road climbing through a long cleft in the hills, which was the upper glen of some notable river. In front was a flat space of maybe a mile, all pitted with bog-holes and rough with tussocks, and then beyond it the road fell steeply down another glen to a plain whose blue dimness melted into the distance. To left and right were round-shouldered green hills as smooth as pancakes, but to the south – that is, the left hand – there was a glimpse of high heathery mountains, which I remembered from the map as the big knot of hill which I had chosen for my sanctuary. I was on the central boss of a huge upland country, and could see everything moving for miles. In the meadows below the road half a mile back a cottage smoked, but it was the only sign of human life. Otherwise there was only the calling of plovers and the tinkling of little streams.

It was now about seven o'clock, and as I waited I heard once again that ominous beat in the air. Then I realised that my vantage-ground might be in reality a trap. There was no cover for a tomtit in those bald green places.

I sat quite still and hopeless while the beat grew louder. Then I saw an aeroplane coming up from the east. It was flying high, but as I looked it dropped several hundred feet and began to circle round the knot of hill in narrowing circles, just as a hawk wheels before it pounces. Now it was flying very low, and now the observer on board caught sight of me. I could see one of the two occupants examining me through glasses.

Suddenly it began to rise in swift whorls, and the next I knew it was speeding eastward again till it became a speck in the blue morning.

That made me do some savage thinking. My enemies had located me, and the next thing would be a cordon round me. I didn't know what force they could command, but I was certain it would be sufficient. The aeroplane had seen my bicycle, and would conclude that I would try to escape by the road. In that case there might be a chance on the moors to the right or left. I wheeled the machine a hundred yards from the highway, and plunged it into a moss-hole where it sank among pond-weed and water-buttercups. Then I climbed to a knoll which gave me a view of the two valleys. Nothing was stirring on the long white ribbon that threaded them.

I have said there was not cover in the whole place to hide a rat. As the day advanced it was flooded with soft fresh light till it had the fragrant sunniness of the South African veld. At other times I would have liked the place, but now it seemed to suffocate me. The free moorlands were prison walls, and the keen hill air was the breath of a dungeon.

I tossed a coin – heads right, tails left – and it fell heads, so I turned to the north. In a little I came to the brow of the ridge which was the containing wall of the pass. I saw the highroad for maybe ten miles, and far down it something that was moving, and that I took to be a motor-car. Beyond the ridge I looked on a rolling green moor, which fell away into wooded glens. Now my life on the veld has given me the eyes of a kite, and I can see things for which most men need a telescope . . . Away down the slope, a couple of miles away, several men were advancing like a row of beaters at a shoot.

I dropped out of sight behind the skyline. That way was shut to me, and I must try the bigger hills to the south beyond the highway. The car I had noticed was getting nearer, but it was still a long way off with some very steep gradients before it. I ran hard, crouching low except in the hollows, and as I ran I kept scanning the brow of the hill before me. Was it imagination, or did I see figures – one, two, perhaps more – moving in a glen beyond the stream?

If you are hemmed in on all sides in a patch of land there is only one chance of escape. You must stay in the patch, and let your enemies search it and not find you. That was good sense, but how on earth was I to escape notice in that table-cloth of a place? I would have buried myself to the neck in mud or lain below water or climbed the tallest tree. But there was not a stick of wood, the bog-holes were little puddles, the stream was a slender trickle. There was nothing but short heather, and bare hill bent, and the white highway.

Then in a tiny bight of road, beside a heap of stones, I found the Roadman.

He had just arrived, and was wearily flinging down his hammer. He looked at me with a fishy eye and yawned.

'Confoond the day I ever left the herdin'!' he said, as if to the world at large. 'There I was my ain maister. Now I'm a slave to the Government, tethered to the roadside, wi' sair een[1] and a back like a suckle.'[2]

He took up the hammer, struck a stone, dropped the implement with an oath, and put both hands to his ears. 'Mercy on me! My heid's burstin'!' he cried.

He was a wild figure, about my own size but much bent, with a week's beard on his chin, and a pair of big horn spectacles.

'I canna dae't,' he cried again. 'The Surveyor maun just report me. I'm for my bed.'

I asked him what was the trouble, though indeed that was clear enough.

'The trouble is that I'm no sober. Last nicht my dochter Merran was waddit,[3] and they danced till fower in the byre. Me and some ither chiels[4] sat down to the drinkin', and here I am. Peety that I ever lookit on the wine when it was red!'

I agreed with him about bed.

'It's easy speakin',' he moaned. 'But I got a post-caird yestreen sayin' that the new Road Surveyor would be round the day. He'll come and he'll no find me, or else he'll find me fou,[5] and either way I'm a done man. I'll awa' back to my bed and say I'm no weel, but I doot that'll no help me, for they ken my kind o' no-weel-ness.'

Then I had an inspiration. 'Does the new Surveyor know you?' I asked.

'No him. He's just been a week at the job. He rins about in a wee motor-cawr, and wad speir[6] the inside oot o' a whelk.'

'Where's your house?' I asked, and was directed by a wavering finger to the cottage by the stream.

'Well, back to your bed,' I said, 'and sleep in peace. I'll take on your job for a bit and see the Surveyor.'

He stared at me blankly; then, as the notion dawned on his fuddled brain, his face broke into the vacant drunkard's smile.

'You're the billy,' he cried. 'It'll be easy eneuch managed. I've finished that bing o' stanes,[7] so you needna chap ony mair this forenoon. Just take the barry, and wheel eneuch metal[8] frae yon quarry doon the road to mak anither bing the morn. My name's Alexander Trummle, and I've been seeven year at the trade, and twenty afore that herdin' on Leithen Water. My freens ca' me Ecky, and whiles Specky, for I wear glesses, being weak i' the sicht. Just you speak the Surveyor fair, and ca' him Sir, and he'll be fell pleased. I'll be back or midday.'

I borrowed his spectacles and filthy old hat; stripped off coat, waistcoat, and collar, and gave him them to carry home; borrowed, too, the foul stump of a clay pipe as an extra property. He indicated my simple tasks, and without more ado set off at an amble bedwards. Bed may have been his chief object, but I think there was also something left in the foot of a bottle. I prayed that he might be safe under cover before my friends arrived on the scene.

Then I set to work to dress for the part. I opened the collar of my shirt – it was a vulgar blue-and-white check such as plough-men wear – and revealed a neck as brown as any tinker's. I rolled up my sleeves, and there was a forearm which might have been a blacksmith's, sunburnt and rough with old scars. I got my boots and trouser-legs all white from the dust of the road, and hitched up my trousers, tying them with string below the knee. Then I set to work on my face. With a handful of dust I made a water-mark round my neck, the place where Mr Turnbull's Sunday ablutions might be expected to stop. I rubbed a good deal of dirt also into the sunburn of my cheeks. A roadman's eyes would no doubt be a little inflamed, so I contrived to get some dust in both of mine, and by dint of vigorous rubbing produced a bleary effect.

The sandwiches Sir Harry had given me had gone off with my coat, but the roadman's lunch, tied up in a red handkerchief, was at my disposal. I ate with great relish several of the thick slabs of scone and cheese and drank a little of the cold tea. In the handkerchief was a local paper tied with string and addressed to Mr Turnbull – obviously meant to solace his midday leisure. I did up the bundle again, and put the paper conspicuously beside it.

My boots did not satisfy me, but by dint of kicking among the stones I reduced them to the granite-like surface which marks a roadman's foot-gear. Then I bit and scraped my finger-nails till the edges were all cracked and uneven. The men I was matched against would miss no detail. I broke one of the bootlaces and retied it in a clumsy knot, and loosed the other so that my thick grey socks bulged over the uppers. Still no sign of anything on the road. The motor I had observed half an hour ago must have gone home.

My toilet complete, I took up the barrow and began my journeys to and from the quarry a hundred yards off.

I remember an old scout in Rhodesia, who had done many queer things in his day, once telling me that the secret of playing a part was to think yourself into it. You could never keep it up, he said, unless you could manage to convince yourself that you were *it*. So I shut off all other thoughts and switched them on to the road-mending. I thought of the little white cottage as my home, I recalled the years I had spent herding on Leithen Water, I made my mind dwell lovingly on sleep in a box-bed and a bottle of cheap whisky. Still nothing appeared on that long white road.

Now and then a sheep wandered off the heather to stare at me. A heron flopped down to a pool in the stream and started to fish, taking no more notice of me than if I had been a milestone. On I went, trundling my loads of stone, with the heavy step of the professional. Soon I grew warm, and the dust on my face changed into solid and abiding grit. I was already counting the hours till evening should put a limit to Mr Turnbull's monotonous toil.

Suddenly a crisp voice spoke from the road, and looking up I saw a little Ford two-seater, and a round-faced young man in a bowler hat.

'Are you Alexander Turnbull?' he asked. 'I am the new County Road Surveyor. You live at Blackhopefoot, and have charge of the section from Laidlawbyres to the Riggs? Good! A fair bit of road, Turnbull, and not badly engineered. A little soft about a mile off, and the edges want cleaning. See you look after that. Good-morning. You'll know me the next time you see me.'

Clearly my get-up was good enough for the dreaded Surveyor. I went on with my work, and as the morning grew towards noon I was cheered by a little traffic. A baker's van breasted the hill, and sold me a bag of ginger biscuits which I stowed in my trouser-pockets against emergencies. Then a herd passed with sheep, and disturbed me somewhat by asking loudly, 'What had become o' Specky?'

'In bed wi' the colic,' I replied, and the herd passed on . . .

Just about midday a big car stole down the hill, glided past and drew up a hundred yards beyond. Its three occupants descended as if to stretch their legs, and sauntered towards me.

Two of the men I had seen before from the window of the Galloway inn – one lean, sharp, and dark, the other comfortable and smiling. The third had the look of a countryman – a vet, perhaps, or a small farmer. He was dressed in ill-cut knicker-bockers, and the eye in his head was as bright and wary as a hen's.

''Morning,' said the last. 'That's a fine easy job o' yours.'

I had not looked up on their approach, and now, when accosted, I slowly and painfully straightened my back, after the manner of roadmen; spat vigorously, after the manner of the low Scot; and regarded them steadily before replying. I confronted three pairs of eyes that missed nothing.

'There's waur jobs and there's better,' I said sententiously. 'I wad rather hae yours, sittin' a' day on your hinderlands on thae cushions. It's you and your muckle[9] cawrs that wreck my roads! If we a' had oor richts, ye sud be made to mend what ye break.'

The bright-eyed man was looking at the newspaper lying beside Turnbull's bundle.

'I see you get your papers in good time,' he said.

I glanced at it casually. 'Aye, in gude time. Seein' that that paper cam' out last Setterday I'm just sax days late.'

He picked it up, glanced at the superscription, and laid it down again. One of the others had been looking at my boots, and a word in German called the speaker's attention to them.

'You've a fine taste in boots,' he said. 'These were never made by a country shoemaker.'

'They were not,' I said readily. 'They were made in London. I got them frae the gentleman that was here last year for the shootin'. What was his name now?' And I scratched a forgetful head.

Again the sleek one spoke in German. 'Let us get on,' he said. 'This fellow is all right.'

They asked one last question.

'Did you see any one pass early this morning? He might be on a bicycle or he might be on foot.'

I very nearly fell into the trap and told a story of a bicyclist hurrying past in the grey dawn. But I had the sense to see my danger. I pretended to consider very deeply.

'I wasna up very early,' I said. 'Ye see, my dochter was merrit last nicht, and we keepit it up late. I opened the house door about seeven and there was naebody on the road then. Since I cam' up here there has just been the baker and the Ruchill herd, besides you gentlemen.'

One of them gave me a cigar, which I smelt gingerly and stuck in Turnbull's bundle. They got into their car and were out of sight in three minutes.

My heart leaped with an enormous relief, but I went on wheeling my stones. It was as well, for ten minutes later the car returned, one of the occupants waving a hand to me. Those gentry left nothing to chance.

I finished Turnbull's bread and cheese, and pretty soon I had finished the stones. The next step was what puzzled me. I could not keep up this road-making business for long. A merciful Providence had kept Mr Turnbull indoors, but if he appeared on the scene there would be trouble. I had a notion that the cordon was still tight round the glen, and that if I walked in any direction I should meet with questioners. But get out I must. No man's nerve could stand more than a day of being spied on.

I stayed at my post till about five o'clock. By that time I had resolved to go down to Turnbull's cottage at nightfall and take my chance of getting over the hills in the darkness. But suddenly a new car came up the road, and slowed down a yard or two from me. A fresh wind had risen, and the occupant wanted to light a cigarette.

It was a touring car, with the tonneau[10] full of an assortment of baggage. One man sat in it, and by an amazing chance I knew him. His name was Marmaduke Jopley, and he was an offence to creation. He was a sort of blood stockbroker, who did his business by toadying eldest sons and rich young peers and foolish old ladies. 'Marmie' was a familiar figure, I understood, at balls and polo-weeks and country houses. He was an adroit scandal-monger, and would crawl a mile on his belly to anything that had a title or a million. I had a business introduction to his firm when I came to London, and he was good enough to ask me to dinner at his club. There he showed off at a great rate, and pattered about his duchesses till the snobbery of the creature turned me sick. I asked a man afterwards why nobody kicked him, and was told that Englishmen reverenced the weaker sex.

Anyhow there he was now, nattily dressed, in a fine new car, obviously on his way to visit some of his smart friends. A sudden daftness took me, and in a second I had jumped into the tonneau and had him by the shoulder.

'Hullo, Jopley,' I sang out. 'Well met, my lad!'

He got a horrid fright. His chin dropped as he stared at me. 'Who the devil are you?' he gasped.

'My name's Hannay,' I said. 'From Rhodesia, you remember.'

'Good God, the murderer!' he choked.

'Just so. And there'll be a second murder, my dear, if you don't do as I tell you. Give me that coat of yours. That cap, too.'

He did as he was bid, for he was blind with terror. Over my dirty trousers and vulgar shirt I put on his smart driving-coat, which buttoned high at the top and thereby hid the deficiencies of my collar. I stuck the cap on my head, and added his gloves to my get up. The dusty roadman in a minute was transformed into one of the neatest motorists in Scotland. On Mr Jopley's head I clapped Turnbull's unspeakable hat, and told him to keep it there.

Then with some difficulty I turned the car. My plan was to go back the road he had come, for the watchers, having seen it before, would probably let it pass unremarked, and Marmie's figure was in no way like mine.

'Now, my child,' I said, 'sit quite still and be a good boy. I mean you no harm. I'm only borrowing your car for an hour or two. But if you play me any tricks, and above all if you open your mouth, as sure as there's a God above me I'll wring your neck. *Savez?*'

I enjoyed that evening's ride. We ran eight miles down the valley, through a village or two, and I could not help noticing several strange-looking folk lounging by the roadside. These were the watchers who would have had much to say to me if I had come in other garb or company. As it was, they looked incuriously on. One touched his cap in salute, and I responded graciously.

As the dark fell I turned up a side glen which, as I remember from the map, led into an unfrequented corner of the hills. Soon the villages were left behind, then the farms, and then even the wayside cottages. Presently we came to a lonely moor where the night was blackening the sunset gleam in the bog pools. Here we stopped, and I obligingly reversed the car and restored to Mr Jopley his belongings.

'A thousand thanks,' I said. 'There's more use in you than I thought. Now be off and find the police.'

As I sat on the hillside, watching the tail light dwindle, I reflected on the various kinds of crime I had now sampled. Contrary to general belief, I was not a murderer, but I had become an unholy liar, a shameless impostor, and a highway-man with a marked taste for expensive motor-cars.

CHAPTER VI
THE ADVENTURE OF THE BALD ARCHAEOLOGIST

I spent the night on a shelf of the hillside, in the lee of a boulder where the heather grew long and soft. It was a cold business, for I had neither coat nor waistcoat. These were in Mr Turnbull's keeping, as was Scudder's little book, my watch and – worst of all – my pipe and tobacco pouch. Only my money accompanied me in my belt, and about half a pound of ginger biscuits in my trousers pocket.

I supped off half those biscuits, and by worming myself deep into the heather got some kind of warmth. My spirits had risen, and I was beginning to enjoy this crazy game of hide-and-seek. So far I had been miraculously lucky. The milkman, the literary innkeeper, Sir Harry, the roadman, and the idiotic Marmie, were all pieces of undeserved good fortune. Somehow the first success gave me a feeling that I was going to pull the thing through.

My chief trouble was that I was desperately hungry. When a Jew shoots himself in the City and there is an inquest, the newspapers usually report that the deceased was 'well-nourished.' I remember thinking that they would not call me well-nourished if I broke my neck in a bog-hole. I lay and tortured myself – for the ginger biscuits merely emphasised the aching void – with the memory of all the good food I had thought so little of in London. There were Paddock's crisp sausages and fragrant shavings of bacon, and shapely poached eggs – how often I had turned up my nose at them! There were the cutlets they did at the club, and a particular ham that stood on the cold table, for which my soul lusted. My thoughts hovered over all varieties of mortal edible, and finally settled on a porter-house steak and a quart of bitter with a welsh rabbit to follow. In longing hopelessly for these dainties I fell asleep.

I woke very cold and stiff about an hour after dawn. It took me a little while to remember where I was, for I had been very weary and had slept heavily. I saw first the pale blue sky through a net of heather, then a big shoulder of hill, and then my own boots placed neatly in a blaeberry[1] bush. I raised myself on my arms and looked down into the valley, and that one look set me lacing up my boots in mad haste.

For there were men below, not more than a quarter of a mile off, spaced out on the hillside like a fan, and beating the heather. Marmie had not been slow in looking for his revenge.

I crawled out of my shelf into the cover of a boulder, and from it gained a shallow trench which slanted up the mountain face. This led me presently into the narrow gully of a burn, by way of which I scrambled to the top of the ridge. From there I looked back, and saw that I was still undiscovered. My pursuers were patiently quartering the hillside and moving upwards.

Keeping behind the skyline I ran for maybe half a mile, till I judged I was above the uppermost end of the glen. Then I showed myself, and was instantly noted by one of the flankers, who passed the word to the others. I heard cries coming up from below, and saw that the line of search had changed its direction. I pretended to retreat over the skyline, but instead went back the way I had come, and in twenty minutes was behind the ridge overlooking my sleeping place. From that view-point I had the satisfaction of seeing the pursuit streaming up the hill at the top of the glen on a hopelessly false scent.

I had before me a choice of routes, and I chose a ridge which made an angle with the one I was on, and so would soon put a deep glen between me and my enemies. The exercise had warmed my blood, and I was beginning to enjoy myself amazingly. As I went I breakfasted on the dusty remnants of the ginger biscuits.

I knew very little about the country, and I hadn't a notion what I was going to do. I trusted to the strength of my legs, but I was well aware that those behind me would be familiar with the lie of the land, and that my ignorance would be a heavy handicap. I saw in front of me a sea of hills, rising very high towards the south, but northwards breaking down into broad ridges which separated wide and shallow dales. The ridge I had chosen seemed to sink after a mile or two to a moor which lay like a pocket in the uplands. That seemed as good a direction to take as any other.

My stratagem had given me a fair start – call it twenty minutes – and I had the width of a glen behind me before I saw the first heads of the pursuers. The police had evidently called in local talent to their aid, and the men I could see had the appearance of herds or gamekeepers. They hallooed at the sight of me, and I waved my hand. Two dived into the glen and began to climb my ridge, while the others kept their own side of the hill. I felt as if I were taking part in a schoolboy game of hare and hounds.

But very soon it began to seem less of a game. Those fellows behind were hefty men on their native heath. Looking back I saw that only three were following direct, and I guessed that the others had fetched a circuit to cut me off. My lack of local knowledge might very well be my undoing, and I resolved to get out of this tangle of glens to the pocket of moor I had seen from the tops. I must so increase my distance as to get clear away from them, and I believed I could do this if I could find the right ground for it. If there had been cover I would have tried a bit of stalking, but on these bare slopes you could see a fly a mile off. My hope must be in the length of my legs and the soundness of my wind, but I needed easier ground for that, for I was not bred a mountaineer. How I longed for a good Afrikander[2] pony!

I put on a great spurt and got off my ridge and down into the moor before any figures appeared on the skyline behind me. I crossed a burn, and came out on a highroad which made a pass between two glens. All in front of me was a big field of heather sloping up to a crest which was crowned with an odd feather of trees. In the dyke by the roadside was a gate, from which a grass-grown track led over the first wave of the moor.

I jumped the dyke and followed it, and after a few hundred yards – as soon as it was out of sight of the highway – the grass stopped and it became a very respectable road, which was evidently kept with some care. Clearly it ran to a house, and I began to think of doing the same. Hitherto my luck had held, and it might be that my best chance would be found in this remote dwelling. Anyhow there were trees there, and that meant cover.

I did not follow the road, but the burnside which flanked it on the right, where the bracken grew deep and the high banks made a tolerable screen. It was well I did so, for no sooner had I gained the hollow than, looking back, I saw the pursuit topping the ridge from which I had descended.

After that I did not look back; I had no time. I ran up the burnside, crawling over the open places, and for a large part wading in the shallow stream. I found a deserted cottage with a row of phantom peat-stacks and an overgrown garden. Then I was among young hay, and very soon had come to the edge of a plantation of wind-blown firs. From there I saw the chimneys of the house smoking a few hundred yards to my left. I forsook the burnside, crossed another dyke, and almost before I knew was on a rough lawn. A glance back told me that I was well out of sight of the pursuit, which had not yet passed the first lift of the moor.

The lawn was a very rough place, cut with a scythe instead of a mower, and planted with beds of scrubby rhododendrons. A brace of black-game,[3] which are not usually garden birds, rose at my approach. The house before me was the ordinary moorland farm, with a more pretentious whitewashed wing added. Attached to this wing was a glass verandah, and through the glass I saw the face of an elderly gentleman meekly watching me.

I stalked over the border of coarse hill gravel and entered the open verandah door. Within was a pleasant room, glass on one side, and on the other a mass of books. More books showed in an inner room. On the floor, instead of tables, stood cases such as you see in a museum, filled with coins and queer stone implements.

There was a knee-hole desk in the middle, and seated at it, with some papers and open volumes before him, was the benevolent old gentleman. His face was round and shiny, like Mr Pickwick's, big glasses were stuck on the end of his nose, and the top of his head was as bright and bare as a glass bottle.

He never moved when I entered, but raised his placid eyebrows and waited on me to speak.

It was not an easy job, with about five minutes to spare, to tell a stranger who I was and what I wanted, and to win his aid. I did not attempt it. There was something about the eye of the man before me, something so keen and knowledgeable, that I could not find a word. I simply stared at him and stuttered.

'You seem in a hurry, my friend,' he said slowly.

I nodded towards the window. It gave a prospect across the moor through a gap in the plantation, and revealed certain figures half a mile off straggling through the heather.

'Ah, I see,' he said, and took up a pair of field-glasses through which he patiently scrutinised the figures.

'A fugitive from justice, eh? Well, we'll go into the matter at our leisure. Meantime I object to my privacy being broken in upon by the clumsy rural policeman. Go into my study, and you will see two doors facing you. Take the one on the left and close it behind you. You will be perfectly safe.'

And this extraordinary man took up his pen again.

I did as I was bid, and found myself in a little dark chamber which smelt of chemicals, and was lit only by a tiny window high up in the wall. The door had swung behind me with a click like the door of a safe. Once again I had found an unexpected sanctuary.

All the same I was not comfortable. There was something about the old gentleman which puzzled and rather terrified me. He had been too easy and ready, almost as if he had expected me. And his eyes had been horribly intelligent.

No sound came to me in that dark place. For all I knew the police might be searching the house, and if they did they would want to know what was behind this door. I tried to possess my soul in patience, and to forget how hungry I was.

Then I took a more cheerful view. The old gentleman could scarcely refuse me a meal, and I fell to reconstructing my breakfast. Bacon and eggs would content me, but I wanted the better part of a flitch of bacon and half a hundred eggs. And then, while my mouth was watering in anticipation, there was a click and the door stood open.

I emerged into the sunlight to find the master of the house sitting in a deep arm-chair in the room he called his study, and regarding me with curious eyes.

'Have they gone?' I asked.

'They have gone. I convinced them that you had crossed the hill. I do not choose that the police should come between me and one whom I am delighted to honour. This is a lucky morning for you, Mr Richard Hannay.'

As he spoke his eyelids seemed to tremble and to fall a little over his keen grey eyes. In a flash the phrase of Scudder's came back to me, when he had described the man he most dreaded in the world. He had said that he 'could hood his eyes like a hawk.' Then I saw that I had walked straight into the enemy's headquarters.

My first impulse was to throttle the old ruffian and make for the open air. He seemed to anticipate my intention, for he smiled gently, and nodded to the door behind me. I turned, and saw two men-servants who had me covered with pistols.

He knew my name, but he had never seen me before. And as the reflection darted across my mind I saw a slender chance.

'I don't know what you mean,' I said roughly. 'And who are you calling Richard Hannay? My name's Ainslie.'

'So?' he said, still smiling. 'But of course you have others. We won't quarrel about a name.'

I was pulling myself together now, and I reflected that my garb, lacking coat and waistcoat and collar, would at any rate not betray me. I put on my surliest face and shrugged my shoulders.

'I suppose you're going to give me up after all, and I call it a damned dirty trick. My God, I wish I had never seen that cursed motor-car! Here's the money and be damned to you,' and I flung four sovereigns on the table.

He opened his eyes a little. 'Oh no, I shall not give you up. My friends and I will have a little private settlement with you, that is all. You know a little too much, Mr Hannay. You are a clever actor, but not quite clever enough.'

He spoke with assurance, but I could see the dawning of a doubt in his mind.

'Oh, for God's sake stop jawing,' I cried. 'Everything's against me. I haven't had a bit of luck since I came on shore at Leith. What's the harm in a poor devil with an empty stomach picking up some money he finds in a bust-up motor-car? That's all I done, and for that I've been chivvied for two days by those blasted bobbies over those blasted hills. I tell you I'm fair sick of it. You can do what you like, old boy! Ned Ainslie's got no fight left in him.'

I could see that the doubt was gaining.

'Will you oblige me with the story of your recent doings?' he asked.

'I can't, guv'nor,' I said in a real beggar's whine. 'I've not had a bite to eat for two days. Give me a mouthful of food, and then you'll hear God's truth.'

I must have showed my hunger in my face, for he signalled to one of the men in the doorway. A bit of cold pie was brought and a glass of beer, and I wolfed them down like a pig – or rather, like Ned Ainslie, for I was keeping up my character. In the middle of my meal he spoke suddenly to me in German, but I turned on him a face as blank as a stone wall.

Then I told him my story – how I had come off an Archangel ship at Leith a week ago, and was making my way overland to my brother at Wigtown. I had run short of cash – I hinted vaguely at a spree – and I was pretty well on my uppers when I had come on a hole in a hedge, and, looking through, had seen a big motor-car lying in the burn. I had poked about to see what had happened, and had found three sovereigns lying on the seat and one on the floor. There was nobody there or any sign of an owner, so I had pocketed the cash. But somehow the law had got after me. When I had tried to change a sovereign in a baker's shop, the woman had cried on the police, and a little later, when I was washing my face in a burn, I had been nearly gripped, and had only got away by leaving my coat and waistcoat behind me.

'They can have the money back,' I cried, 'for a fat lot of good it's done me. Those perishers are all down on a poor man. Now, if it had been you, guv'nor, that had found the quids, nobody would have troubled you.'

'You're a good liar, Hannay,' he said.

I flew into a rage. 'Stop fooling, damn you! I tell you my name's Ainslie, and I never heard of any one called Hannay in my born days. I'd sooner have the police than you with your Hannays and your monkey-faced pistol tricks . . . No, guv'nor, I beg pardon, I don't mean that. I'm much obliged to you for the grub, and I'll thank you to let me go now the coast's clear.'

It was obvious that he was badly puzzled. You see he had never seen me, and my appearance must have altered considerably from my photographs, if he had got one of them. I was pretty smart and well dressed in London, and now I was a regular tramp.

'I do not propose to let you go. If you are what you say you are, you will soon have a chance of clearing yourself. If you are what I believe you are, I do not think you will see the light much longer.'

He rang a bell, and a third servant appeared from the verandah.

'I want the Lanchester[4] in five minutes,' he said. 'There will be three to luncheon.'

Then he looked steadily at me, and that was the hardest ordeal of all.

There was something weird and devilish in those eyes, cold, malignant, unearthly, and most hellishly clever. They fascinated me like the bright eyes of a snake. I had a strong impulse to throw myself on his mercy and offer to join his side, and if you consider the way I felt about the whole thing you will see that that impulse must have been purely physical, the weakness of a brain mesmerised and mastered by a stronger spirit. But I managed to stick it out and even to grin.

'You'll know me next time, guv'nor,' I said.

'Karl,' he spoke in German to one of the men in the doorway, 'you will put this fellow in the storeroom till I return, and you will be answerable to me for his keeping.'

I was marched out of the room with a pistol at each ear.

The storeroom was a damp chamber in what had been the old farmhouse. There was no carpet on the uneven floor, and nothing to sit down on but a school form. It was black as pitch, for

the windows were heavily shuttered. I made out by groping that
the walls were lined with boxes and barrels and sacks of some
heavy stuff. The whole place smelt of mould and disuse. My
gaolers turned the key in the door, and I could hear them shifting
their feet as they stood on guard outside.

I sat down in that chilly darkness in a very miserable frame
of mind. The old boy had gone off in a motor to collect the two
ruffians who had interviewed me yesterday. Now, they had seen
me as the roadman, and they would remember me, for I was in
the same rig. What was a roadman doing twenty miles from his
beat, pursued by the police? A question or two would put them
on the track. Probably they had seen Mr Turnbull, probably
Marmie too; most likely they could link me up with Sir Harry,
and then the whole thing would be crystal clear. What chance
had I in this moorland house with three desperadoes and their
armed servants?

I began to think wistfully of the police, now plodding
over the hills after my wraith. They at any rate were fellow-
countrymen and honest men, and their tender mercies would be
kinder than these ghoulish aliens. But they wouldn't have
listened to me. That old devil with the eyelids had not taken
long to get rid of them. I thought he probably had some kind of
graft with the constabulary. Most likely he had letters from
Cabinet Ministers saying he was to be given every facility for
plotting against Britain. That's the sort of owlish way we run
our politics in the Old Country.

The three would be back for lunch, so I hadn't more than a
couple of hours to wait. It was simply waiting on destruction,
for I could see no way out of this mess. I wished that I had
Scudder's courage, for I am free to confess I didn't feel any
great fortitude. The only thing that kept me going was that I
was pretty furious. It made me boil with rage to think of those
three spies getting the pull on me like this. I hoped that at any
rate I might be able to twist one of their necks before they
downed me.

The more I thought of it the angrier I grew, and I had to get
up and move about the room. I tried the shutters, but they were
the kind that lock with a key, and I couldn't move them. From

the outside came the faint clucking of hens in the warm sun. Then I groped among the sacks and boxes. I couldn't open the latter, and the sacks seemed to be full of things like dog-biscuits that smelt of cinnamon. But, as I circumnavigated the room, I found a handle in the wall which seemed worth investigating.

It was the door of a wall cupboard – what they call a 'press' in Scotland – and it was locked. I shook it, and it seemed rather flimsy. For want of something better to do I put out my strength on that door, getting some purchase on the handle by looping my braces round it. Presently the thing gave with a crash which I thought would bring in my warders to inquire. I waited for a bit, and then started to explore the cupboard shelves.

There was a multitude of queer things there. I found an odd vesta or two in my trouser pockets and struck a light. It went out in a second, but it showed me one thing. There was a little stock of electric torches on one shelf. I picked up one, and found it was in working order.

With the torch to help me I investigated further. There were bottles and cases of queer-smelling stuffs, chemicals no doubt for experiments, and there were coils of fine copper wire and yanks and yanks of a thin oiled silk. There was a box of detonators, and a lot of cord for fuses. Then away at the back of a shelf I found a stout brown cardboard box, and inside it a wooden case. I managed to wrench it open, and within lay half a dozen little grey bricks, each a couple of inches square.

I took up one, and found that it crumbled easily in my hand. Then I smelt it and put my tongue to it. After that I sat down to think. I hadn't been a mining engineer for nothing, and I knew lentonite[5] when I saw it.

With one of these bricks I could blow the house to smithereens. I had used the stuff in Rhodesia and knew its power. But the trouble was that my knowledge wasn't exact. I had forgotten the proper charge and the right way of preparing it, and I wasn't sure about the timing. I had only a vague notion, too, as to its power, for though I had used it I had not handled it with my own fingers.

But it was a chance, the only possible chance. It was a mighty risk, but against it was an absolute black certainty. If I used it the odds were, as I reckoned, about five to one in favour of my blowing myself into the tree-tops; but if I didn't I should very likely be occupying a six-foot hole in the garden by the evening. That was the way I had to look at it. The prospect was pretty dark either way, but anyhow there was a chance, both for myself and for my country.

The remembrance of little Scudder decided me. It was about the beastliest moment of my life, for I'm no good at these cold-blooded resolutions. Still I managed to rake up the pluck to set my teeth and choke back the horrid doubts that flooded in on me. I simply shut off my mind and pretended I was doing an experiment as simple as Guy Fawkes fireworks.

I got a detonator, and fixed it to a couple of feet of fuse. Then I took a quarter of a lentonite brick, and buried it near the door below one of the sacks in a crack of the floor, fixing the detonator in it. For all I knew half those boxes might be dynamite. If the cupboard held such deadly explosives, why not the boxes? In that case there would be a glorious skyward journey for me and the German servants and about an acre of the surrounding country. There was also the risk that the detonation might set off the other bricks in the cupboard, for I had forgotten most that I knew about lentonite. But it didn't do to begin thinking about the possibilities. The odds were horrible, but I had to take them.

I ensconced myself just below the sill of the window, and lit the fuse. Then I waited for a moment or two. There was dead silence – only a shuffle of heavy boots in the passage, and the peaceful cluck of hens from the warm out-of-doors. I commended my soul to my Maker, and wondered where I would be in five seconds . . .

A great wave of heat seemed to surge upwards from the floor, and hang for a blistering instant in the air. Then the wall opposite me flashed into a golden yellow and dissolved with a rending thunder that hammered my brain into a pulp. Something dropped on me, catching the point of my left shoulder.

And then I think I became unconscious.

My stupor can scarcely have lasted beyond a few seconds. I felt myself being choked by thick yellow fumes, and struggled out of the debris to my feet. Somewhere behind me I felt fresh air. The jambs of the window had fallen, and through the ragged rent the smoke was pouring out to the summer noon. I stepped over the broken lintel, and found myself standing in a yard in a dense and acrid fog. I felt very sick and ill, but I could move my limbs, and I staggered blindly forward away from the house.

A small mill-lade[6] ran in a wooden aqueduct at the other side of the yard, and into this I fell. The cool water revived me, and I had just enough wits left to think of escape. I squirmed up the lade among the slippery green slime till I reached the mill-wheel. Then I wriggled through the axle hole into the old mill and tumbled on to a bed of chaff. A nail caught the seat of my trousers, and I left a wisp of heather-mixture behind me.

The mill had been long out of use. The ladders were rotten with age, and in the loft the rats had gnawed great holes in the floor. Nausea shook me, and a wheel in my head kept turning, while my left shoulder and arm seemed to be stricken with the palsy. I looked out of the window and saw a fog still hanging over the house and smoke escaping from an upper window. Please God I had set the place on fire, for I could hear confused cries coming from the other side.

But I had no time to linger, since this mill was obviously a bad hiding-place. Any one looking for me would naturally follow the lade, and I made certain the search would begin as soon as they found that my body was not in the storeroom. From another window I saw that on the far side of the mill stood an old stone dovecot. If I could get there without leaving tracks I might find a hiding-place, for I argued that my enemies, if they thought I could move, would conclude I had made for open country, and would go seeking me on the moor.

I crawled down the broken ladder, scattering chaff behind me to cover my footsteps. I did the same on the mill floor, and on the threshold where the door hung on broken hinges. Peeping out, I saw that between me and the dovecot was a piece of bare cobbled ground, where no footmarks would show. Also it was mercifully hid by the mill buildings from any view from the house. I slipped across the space, got to the back of the dovecot and prospected a way of ascent.

That was one of the hardest jobs I ever took on. My shoulder and arm ached like hell, and I was so sick and giddy that I was always on the verge of falling. But I managed it somehow. By the use of out-jutting stones and gaps in the masonry and a tough ivy root I got to the top in the end. There was a little parapet behind which I found space to lie down. Then I proceeded to go off into an old-fashioned swoon.

I woke with a burning head and the sun glaring in my face. For a long time I lay motionless, for those horrible fumes seemed to have loosened my joints and dulled my brain. Sounds came to me from the house – men speaking throatily and the throbbing of a stationary car. There was a little gap in the parapet to which I wriggled, and from which I had some sort of prospect of the yard. I saw figures come out – a servant with his head bound up, and then a younger man in knickerbockers. They were looking for something, and moved towards the mill. Then one of them caught sight of the wisp of cloth on the nail, and cried out to the other. They both went back to the house, and brought two more to look at it. I saw the rotund figure of my late captor, and I thought I made out the man with the lisp. I noticed that all had pistols.

For half an hour they ransacked the mill. I could hear them kicking over the barrels and pulling up the rotten planking. Then they came outside, and stood just below the dovecot, arguing fiercely. The servant with the bandage was being soundly rated. I heard them fiddling with the door of the dovecot, and for one horrid moment I fancied they were coming up. Then they thought better of it, and went back to the house.

All that long blistering afternoon I lay baking on the roof-top. Thirst was my chief torment. My tongue was like a stick, and to make it worse I could hear the cool drip of water from the mill-lade. I watched the course of the little stream as it came in from the moor, and my fancy followed it to the top of the glen, where it must issue from an icy fountain fringed with cool ferns and mosses. I would have given a thousand pounds to plunge my face into that.

I had a fine prospect of the whole ring of moorland. I saw the car speed away with two occupants, and a man on a hill pony riding east. I judged they were looking for me, and I wished them joy of their quest.

But I saw something else more interesting. The house stood almost on the summit of a swell of moorland which crowned a sort of plateau, and there was no higher point nearer than the big hills six miles off. The actual summit, as I have mentioned, was a biggish clump of trees – firs mostly, with a few ashes and beeches. On the dovecot I was almost on a level with the tree-tops, and could see what lay beyond. The wood was not solid, but only a ring, and inside was an oval of green turf, for all the world like a big cricket-field.

I didn't take long to guess what it was. It was an aerodrome, and a secret one. The place had been most cunningly chosen. For suppose any one were watching an aeroplane descending here, he would think it had gone over the hill beyond the trees. As the place was on the top of a rise in the midst of a big amphitheatre, any observer from any direction would conclude it had passed out of view behind the hill. Only a man very close at hand would realise that the aeroplane had not gone over but had descended in the midst of the wood. An observer with a telescope on one of the higher hills might have discovered the truth, but only herds went there, and herds do not carry spy-glasses. When I looked from the dovecot I could see far away a blue line which I knew was the sea, and I grew furious to think that our enemies had this secret conning-tower to rake our waterways.

Then I reflected that if that aeroplane came back the chances were ten to one that I would be discovered. So through the afternoon I lay and prayed for the coming of darkness, and glad I was when the sun went down over the big western hills and the twilight haze crept over the moor. The aeroplane was late. The gloaming was far advanced when I heard the beat of wings and saw it vol-planing[7] downward to its home in the wood. Lights twinkled for a bit and there was much coming and going from the house. Then the dark fell, and silence.

Thank God it was a black night. The moon was well on its last quarter and would not rise till late. My thirst was too great to allow me to tarry, so about nine o'clock, so far as I could judge, I started to descend. It wasn't easy, and half-way down I heard the back-door of the house open, and saw the gleam of a lantern against the mill wall. For some agonising minutes I hung by the ivy and prayed that whoever it was would not come round by the dovecot. Then the light disappeared, and I dropped as softly as I could on to the hard soil of the yard.

I crawled on my belly in the lee of a stone dyke till I reached the fringe of trees which surrounded the house. If I had known how to do it I would have tried to put that aeroplane out of action, but I realised that any attempt would probably be futile. I was pretty certain that there would be some kind of defence round the house, so I went through the wood on hands and knees, feeling carefully every inch before me. It was as well, for presently I came on a wire about two feet from the ground. If I had tripped over that, it would doubtless have rung some bell in the house and I would have been captured.

A hundred yards farther on I found another wire cunningly placed on the edge of a small stream. Beyond that lay the moor, and in five minutes I was deep in bracken and heather. Soon I was round the shoulder of the rise, in the little glen from which the mill-lade flowed. Ten minutes later my face was in the spring, and I was soaking down pints of the blessed water.

But I did not stop till I had put half a dozen miles between me and that accursed dwelling.

CHAPTER VII
THE DRY-FLY FISHERMAN

I sat down on a hill-top and took stock of my position. I wasn't feeling very happy, for my natural thankfulness at my escape was clouded by my severe bodily discomfort. Those lentonite fumes had fairly poisoned me, and the baking hours on the dovecot hadn't helped matters. I had a crushing headache, and felt as sick as a cat. Also my shoulder was in a bad way. At first I thought it was only a bruise, but it seemed to be swelling, and I had no use of my left arm.

My plan was to seek Mr Turnbull's cottage, recover my garments, and especially Scudder's note-book, and then make for the main line and get back to the south. It seemed to me that the sooner I got in touch with the Foreign Office man, Sir Walter Bullivant, the better. I didn't see how I could get more proof than I had got already. He must just take or leave my story, and anyway, with him I would be in better hands than those devilish Germans. I had begun to feel quite kindly towards the British police.

It was a wonderful starry night, and I had not much difficulty about the road. Sir Harry's map had given me the lie of the land, and all I had to do was to steer a point or two west of south-west to come to the stream where I had met the roadman. In all these travels I never knew the names of the places, but I believe this stream was no less than the upper waters of the river Tweed. I calculated I must be about eighteen miles distant, and that meant I could not get there before morning. So I must lie up a day somewhere, for I was too outrageous a figure to be seen in the sunlight. I had neither coat, waistcoat, collar, nor hat, my trousers were badly torn, and my face and hands were black with the explosion. I daresay I had other beauties, for my eyes felt as if they were furiously bloodshot. Altogether I was no spectacle for God-fearing citizens to see on a highroad.

Very soon after daybreak I made an attempt to clean myself in a hill burn, and then approached a herd's cottage, for I was feeling the need of food. The herd was away from home, and his wife was alone, with no neighbour for five miles. She was a decent old body, and a plucky one, for though she got a fright when she saw me, she had an axe handy, and would have used it on any evil-doer. I told her that I had had a fall – I didn't say how – and she saw by my looks that I was pretty sick. Like a true Samaritan she asked no questions, but gave me a bowl of milk with a dash of whisky in it, and let me sit for a little by her kitchen fire. She would have bathed my shoulder, but it ached so badly that I would not let her touch it.

I don't know what she took me for – a repentant burglar, perhaps; for when I wanted to pay her for the milk and tendered a sovereign, which was the smallest coin I had, she shook her head and said something about 'giving it to them that had a right to it.' At this I protested so strongly that I think she believed me honest, for she took the money and gave me a warm new plaid for it, and an old hat of her man's. She showed me how to wrap the plaid round my shoulders, and when I left that cottage I was the living image of the kind of Scotsman you see in the illustrations to Burns's poems. But at any rate I was more or less clad.

It was as well, for the weather changed before midday to a thick drizzle of rain. I found shelter below an overhanging rock in the crook of a burn, where a drift of dead brackens made a tolerable bed. There I managed to sleep till nightfall, waking very cramped and wretched, with my shoulder gnawing like a toothache. I ate the oat-cake and cheese the old wife had given me, and set out again just before the darkening.

I pass over the miseries of that night among the wet hills. There were no stars to steer by, and I had to do the best I could from my memory of the map. Twice I lost my way, and I had some nasty falls into peat-bogs. I had only about ten miles to go as the crow flies, but my mistakes made it nearer twenty. The last bit was completed with set teeth and a very light and dizzy head. But I managed it, and in the early dawn I was knocking at Mr Turnbull's door. The mist lay close and thick, and from the cottage I could not see the highroad.

Mr Turnbull himself opened to me – sober and something more than sober. He was primly dressed in an ancient but well-tended suit of black; he had been shaved not later than the night before; he wore a linen collar; and in his left hand he carried a pocket Bible. At first he did not recognise me.

'Whae are ye that comes stravaigin'[1] here on the Sabbath mornin'?' he asked.

I had lost all count of the days. So the Sabbath was the reason for his strange decorum.

My head was swimming so wildly that I could not frame a coherent answer. But he recognised me, and he saw that I was ill.

'Hae ye got my specs?' he asked.

I fetched them out of my trouser pocket and gave him them.

'Ye'll hae come for your jaicket and westcoat,' he said. 'Come in-bye. Losh, man, ye're terrible dune i' the legs. Haud up till I get ye to a chair.'

I perceived I was in for a bout of malaria. I had a good deal of fever in my bones, and the wet night had brought it out, while my shoulder and the effects of the fumes combined to make me feel pretty bad. Before I knew, Mr Turnbull was helping me off with my clothes, and putting me to bed in one of the two cupboards that lined the kitchen walls.

He was a true friend in need, that old roadman. His wife was dead years ago, and since his daughter's marriage he lived alone. For the better part of ten days he did all the rough nursing I needed. I simply wanted to be left in peace while the fever took its course, and when my skin was cool again I found that the bout had more or less cured my shoulder. But it was a baddish go, and though I was out of bed in five days, it took me some time to get my legs again.

He went out each morning, leaving me milk for the day, and locking the door behind him; and came in in the evening to sit silent in the chimney corner. Not a soul came near the place. When I was getting better, he never bothered me with a question.

Several times he fetched me a two-days' old *Scotsman*, and I noticed that the interest in the Portland Place murder seemed to have died down. There was no mention of it, and I could find very little about anything except a thing called the General Assembly[2] – some ecclesiastical spree, I gathered.

One day he produced my belt from a lockfast drawer. 'There's a terrible heap o'siller[3] in't,' he said. 'Ye'd better coont it to see it's a' there.'

He never even sought my name. I asked him if anybody had been around making inquiries subsequent to my spell at the roadmaking.

'Ay, there was a man in a motor-cawr. He speired whae had ta'en my place that day, and I let on I thocht him daft. But he keepit on at me, and syne I said he maun be thinkin' o' my gude-brither[4] frae the Cleuch[5] that whiles lent me a haun'. He was a wersh-lookin' sowl,[6] and I couldna understand the half o' his English tongue.'

I was getting pretty restless those last days, and as soon as I felt myself fit I decided to be off. That was not till the twelfth day of June, and as luck would have it a drover went past that morning taking some cattle to Moffat. He was a man named Hislop, a friend of Turnbull's, and he came in to his breakfast with us and offered to take me with him.

I made Turnbull accept five pounds for my lodging, and a hard job I had of it. There never was a more independent being. He grew positively rude when I pressed him, and shy and red, and took the money at last without a thank you. When I told him how much I owed him, he grunted something about 'ae guid turn deservin' anither.' You would have thought from our leave-taking that we had parted in disgust.

Hislop was a cheery soul, who chattered all the way over the pass and down the sunny vale of Annan. I talked of Galloway markets and sheep prices, and he made up his mind I was a 'pack-shepherd' from those parts – whatever that may be. My plaid and my old hat, as I have said, gave me a fine theatrical Scots look. But driving cattle is a mortally slow job, and we took the better part of the day to cover a dozen miles.

If I had not had such an anxious heart I would have enjoyed

that time. It was shining blue weather, with a constantly chang-
ing prospect of brown hills and far green meadows, and a
continual sound of larks and curlews and falling streams. But I
had no mind for the summer, and little for Hislop's conver-
sation, for as the fateful fifteenth of June drew near I was
overweighed with the hopeless difficulties of my enterprise.

I got some dinner in a humble Moffat public-house, and
walked the two miles to the junction on the main line. The night
express for the south was not due till near midnight, and to fill
up the time I went up on the hillside and fell asleep, for the walk
had tired me. I all but slept too long, and had to run to the
station and catch the train with two minutes to spare. The feel
of the hard third-class cushions and the smell of stale tobacco
cheered me up wonderfully. At any rate, I felt now that I was
getting to grips with my job.

I was decanted at Crewe in the small hours and had to wait till
six to get a train for Birmingham. In the afternoon I got to
Reading, and changed into a local train which journeyed into
the deeps of Berkshire. Presently I was in a land of lush water-
meadows and slow reedy streams. About eight o'clock in the
evening, a weary and travelled-stained being – a cross between
a farm-labourer and a vet – with a checked black-and-white
plaid over his arm (for I did not dare to wear it south of the
Border), descended at the little station of Artinswell. There were
several people on the platform, and I thought I had better wait
to ask my way till I was clear of the place.

The road led through a wood of great beeches and then into
a shallow valley, with the green backs of downs peeping over
the distant trees. After Scotland the air smelt heavy and flat, but
infinitely sweet, for the limes and chestnuts and lilac bushes
were domes of blossom. Presently I came to a bridge, below
which a clear slow stream flowed between snowy beds of water-
buttercups. A little above it was a mill; and the lasher[7] made a
pleasant cool sound in the scented dusk. Somehow the place
soothed me and put me at my ease. I fell to whistling as I looked
into the green depths, and the tune which came to my lips was
'Annie Laurie.'

A fisherman came up from the water-side, and as he neared me he too began to whistle. The tune was infectious, for he followed my suit. He was a huge man in untidy old flannels and a wide-brimmed hat, with a canvas bag slung on his shoulder. He nodded to me, and I thought I had never seen a shrewder or better-tempered face. He leaned his delicate ten-foot split-cane rod against the bridge, and looked with me at the water.

'Clear, isn't it?' he said pleasantly. 'I back our Kennet any day against the Test. Look at that big fellow. Four pounds if he's an ounce. But the evening rise is over and you can't tempt 'em.'

'I don't see him,' said I.

'Look! There! A yard from the reeds just above that stickle.'

'I've got him now. You might swear he was a black stone.'

'So,' he said, and whistled another bar of 'Annie Laurie.'

'Twisdon's the name, isn't it?' he said over his shoulder, his eyes still fixed on the stream.

'No,' I said. 'I mean to say, Yes.' I had forgotten all about my *alias*.

'It's a wise conspirator that knows his own name,' he observed, grinning broadly at a moor-hen that emerged from the bridge's shadow.

I stood up and looked at him, at the square, cleft jaw and broad, lined brow and the firm folds of cheek, and began to think that here at last was an ally worth having. His whimsical blue eyes seemed to go very deep.

Suddenly he frowned. 'I call it disgraceful,' he said, raising his voice. 'Disgraceful that an able-bodied man like you should dare to beg. You can get a meal from my kitchen, but you'll get no money from me.'

A dog-cart was passing, driven by a young man who raised his whip to salute the fisherman. When he had gone, he picked up his rod.

'That's my house,' he said, pointing to a white gate a hundred yards on. 'Wait five minutes and then go round to the back door.' And with that he left me.

I did as I was bidden. I found a pretty cottage with a lawn running down to the stream, and a perfect jungle of guelder-rose and lilac flanking the path. The back door stood open, and a grave butler was awaiting me.

'Come this way, sir,' he said, and he led me along a passage and up a back staircase to a pleasant bedroom looking towards the river. There I found a complete outfit laid out for me – dress clothes with all the fixings, a brown flannel suit, shirts, collars, ties, shaving things and hair-brushes, even a pair of patent shoes. 'Sir Walter thought as how Mr Reggie's things would fit you, sir,' said the butler. 'He keeps some clothes 'ere, for he comes regular on the week-ends. There's a bathroom next door, and I've prepared a 'ot bath. Dinner in 'alf an hour, sir. You'll 'ear the gong.'

The grave being withdrew, and I sat down in a chintz-covered easy-chair and gaped. It was like a pantomime, to come suddenly out of beggardom into this orderly comfort. Obviously Sir Walter believed in me, though why he did I could not guess. I looked at myself in the mirror and saw a wild, haggard brown fellow, with a fortnight's ragged beard, and dust in ears and eyes, collarless, vulgarly shirted, with shapeless old tweed clothes and boots that had not been cleaned for the better part of a month. I made a fine tramp and a fair drover; and here I was ushered by a prim butler into this temple of gracious ease. And the best of it was that they did not even know my name.

I resolved not to puzzle my head but to take the gifts the gods had provided. I shaved and bathed luxuriously, and got into the dress clothes and clean crackling shirt, which fitted me not so badly. By the time I had finished the looking-glass showed a not unpersonable young man.

Sir Walter awaited me in a dusky dining-room where a little round table was lit with silver candles. The sight of him – so respectable and established and secure, the embodiment of law and government and all the conventions – took me aback and made me feel an interloper. He couldn't know the truth about me, or he wouldn't treat me like this. I simply could not accept his hospitality on false pretences.

'I'm more obliged to you than I can say, but I'm bound to make things clear,' I said. 'I'm an innocent man, but I'm wanted by the police. I've got to tell you this, and I won't be surprised if you kick me out.'

He smiled. 'That's all right. Don't let that interfere with your appetite. We can talk about these things after dinner.'

I never ate a meal with greater relish, for I had had nothing all day but railway sandwiches. Sir Walter did me proud, for we drank a good champagne and had some uncommon fine port afterwards. It made me almost hysterical to be sitting there, waited on by a footman and a sleek butler, and remember that I had been living for three weeks like a brigand, with every man's hand against me. I told Sir Walter about tiger-fish in the Zambesi that bite off your fingers if you give them a chance, and we discussed sport up and down the globe, for he had hunted a bit in his day.

We went to his study for coffee, a jolly room full of books and trophies and untidiness and comfort. I made up my mind that if ever I got rid of this business and had a house of my own, I would create just such a room. Then when the coffee-cups were cleared away, and we had got our cigars alight, my host swung his long legs over the side of his chair and bade me get started with my yarn.

'I've obeyed Harry's instructions,' he said, 'and the bribe he offered me was that you would tell me something to wake me up. I'm ready, Mr Hannay.'

I noticed with a start that he called me by my proper name.

I began at the very beginning. I told of my boredom in London, and the night I had come back to find Scudder gibbering on my doorstep. I told him all Scudder had told me about Karolides and the Foreign Office conference, and that made him purse his lips and grin. Then I got to the murder, and he grew solemn again. He heard all about the milkman and my time in Galloway, and my deciphering Scudder's notes at the inn.

'You've got them here?' he asked sharply, and drew a long breath when I whipped the little book from my pocket.

I said nothing of the contents. Then I described my meeting with Sir Harry, and the speeches at the hall. At that he laughed uproariously.

'Harry talked dashed nonsense, did he? I quite believe it. He's as good a chap as ever breathed, but his idiot of an uncle has stuffed his head with maggots. Go on, Mr Hannay.'

My day as roadman excited him a bit. He made me describe the two fellows in the car very closely, and seemed to be raking back in his memory. He grew merry again when he heard of the fate of that ass Jopley.

But the old man in the moorland house solemnised him. Again I had to describe every detail of his appearance.

'Bland and bald-headed and hooded his eyes like a bird . . . He sounds a sinister wild-fowl! And you dynamited his hermitage, after he had saved you from the police. Spirited piece of work, that!'

Presently I reached the end of my wanderings. He got up slowly, and looked down at me from the hearth-rug.

'You may dismiss the police from your mind,' he said. 'You're in no danger from the law of this land.'

'Great Scot!' I cried. 'Have they got the murderer?'

'No. But for the last fortnight they have dropped you from the list of possibles.'

'Why?' I asked in amazement.

'Principally because I received a letter from Scudder. I knew something of the man, and he did several jobs for me. He was half crank, half genius, but he was wholly honest. The trouble about him was his partiality for playing a lone hand. That made him pretty well useless in any Secret Service – a pity, for he had uncommon gifts. I think he was the bravest man in the world, for he was always shivering with fright, and yet nothing would choke him off. I had a letter from him on the 31st of May.'

'But he had been dead a week by then.'

'The letter was written and posted on the 23rd. He evidently did not anticipate an immediate decease. His communications usually took a week to reach me, for they were sent under cover to Spain and then to Newcastle. He had a mania, you know, for concealing his tracks.'

'What did he say?' I stammered.

'Nothing. Merely that he was in danger, but had found shelter with a good friend, and that I would hear from him before the 15th of June. He gave me no address, but said he was living near

Portland Place. I think his object was to clear you if anything happened. When I got it I went to Scotland Yard, went over the details of the inquest, and concluded that you were the friend. We made inquiries about you, Mr Hannay, and found you were respectable. I thought I knew the motives for your disappearance – not only the police, the other one too – and when I got Harry's scrawl I guessed at the rest. I have been expecting you any time this past week.'

You can imagine what a load this took off my mind. I felt a free man once more, for I was now up against my country's enemies only, and not my country's law.

'Now let us have the little note-book,' said Sir Walter.

It took us a good hour to work through it. I explained the cypher, and he was jolly quick at picking it up. He emended my reading of it on several points, but I had been fairly correct, on the whole. His face was very grave before he had finished, and he sat silent for a while.

'I don't know what to make of it,' he said at last. 'He is right about one thing – what is going to happen the day after to-morrow. How the devil can it have got known? That is ugly enough in itself. But all this about war and the Black Stone – it reads like some wild melodrama. If only I had more confidence in Scudder's judgment. The trouble about him was that he was too romantic. He had the artistic temperament, and wanted a story to be better than God meant it to be. He had a lot of odd biases, too. Jews, for example, made him see red. Jews and the high finance.

'The Black Stone,' he repeated. '*Der Schwarzestein*. It's like a penny novelette. And all this stuff about Karolides. That is the weak part of the tale, for I happen to know that the virtuous Karolides is likely to outlast us both. There is no State in Europe that wants him gone. Besides, he has just been playing up to Berlin and Vienna and giving my Chief some uneasy moments. No! Scudder has gone off the track there. Frankly, Hannay, I don't believe that part of his story. There's some nasty business afoot, and he found out too much and lost his life over it. But I am ready to take my oath that it is ordinary spy work. A certain great European Power makes a hobby of her spy system, and her methods are not too particular. Since she pays by piece-work her blackguards are not likely to stick at a murder or two. They want our naval dispositions for their collection at the Marineamt;[8] but they will be pigeon-holed – nothing more.'

Just then the butler entered the room.

'There's a trunk-call from London, Sir Walter. It's Mr 'Eath, and he wants to speak to you personally.'

My host went off to the telephone.

He returned in five minutes with a whitish face. 'I apologise to the shade of Scudder,' he said. 'Karolides was shot dead this evening at a few minutes after seven.'

CHAPTER VIII
THE COMING OF THE BLACK STONE

I came down to breakfast next morning, after eight hours of blessed dreamless sleep, to find Sir Walter decoding a telegram in the midst of muffins and marmalade. His fresh rosyness of yesterday seemed a thought tarnished.

'I had a busy hour on the telephone after you went to bed,' he said. 'I got my Chief to speak to the First Lord[1] and the Secretary for War, and they are bringing Royer over a day sooner. This wire clinches it. He will be in London at five. Odd that the code word for a *Sous-chef d'Etat Major-General*[2] should be "Porker."'

He directed me to the hot dishes and went on.

'Not that I think it will do much good. If your friends were clever enough to find out the first arrangement they are clever enough to discover the change. I would give my head to know where the leak is. We believed there were only five men in England who knew about Royer's visit, and you may be certain there were fewer in France, for they manage these things better there.'

While I ate he continued to talk, making me to my surprise a present of his full confidence.

'Can the dispositions not be changed?' I asked.

'They could,' he said. 'But we want to avoid that if possible. They are the result of immense thought, and no alteration would be as good. Besides, on one or two points change is simply impossible. Still, something could be done, I suppose, if it were absolutely necessary. But you see the difficulty, Hannay. Our enemies are not going to be such fools as to pick Royer's pocket or any childish game like that. They know that would mean a row and put us on our guard. Their aim is to get the details without any one of us knowing, so that Royer will go back to Paris in the belief that the whole business is still deadly secret. If they can't do that they fail, for, once we suspect, they know that the whole thing must be altered.'

'Then we must stick by the Frenchman's side till he is home again,' I said. 'If they thought they could get the information in Paris they would try there. It means that they have some deep scheme on foot in London which they reckon is going to win out.'

'Royer dines with my Chief, and then comes to my house where four people will see him – Whittaker from the Admiralty, myself, Sir Arthur Drew, and General Winstanley. The First Lord is ill, and has gone to Sherringham. At my house he will get a certain document from Whittaker, and after that he will be motored to Portsmouth where a destroyer will take him to Havre. His journey is too important for the ordinary boat-train. He will never be left unattended for a moment till he is safe on French soil. The same with Whittaker till he meets Royer. That is the best we can do, and it's hard to see how there can be any miscarriage. But I don't mind admitting that I'm horribly nervous. This murder of Karolides will play the deuce in the chancelleries of Europe.'

After breakfast he asked me if I could drive a car.

'Well, you'll be my chauffeur to-day and wear Hudson's rig. You're about his size. You have a hand in this business and we are taking no risks. There are desperate men against us, who will not respect the country retreat of an overworked official.'

When I first came to London I had bought a car and amused myself with running about the south of England, so I knew something of the geography. I took Sir Walter to town by the Bath Road and made good going. It was a soft breathless June morning, with a promise of sultriness later, but it was delicious enough swinging through the little towns with their freshly watered streets, and past the summer gardens of the Thames valley. I landed Sir Walter at his house in Queen Anne's Gate punctually by half-past eleven. The butler was coming up by train with the luggage.

The first thing he did was to take me round to Scotland Yard. There we saw a prim gentleman, with a clean-shaven, lawyer's face.

'I've brought you the Portland Place murderer,' was Sir Walter's introduction.

The reply was a wry smile. 'It would have been a welcome present, Bullivant. This, I presume, is Mr Richard Hannay, who for some days greatly interested my department.'

'Mr Hannay will interest it again. He has much to tell you, but not to-day. For certain grave reasons his tale must wait for twenty-four hours. Then, I can promise you, you will be entertained and possibly edified. I want you to assure Mr Hannay that he will suffer no further inconvenience.'

This assurance was promptly given. 'You can take up your life where you left off,' I was told. 'Your flat, which probably you no longer wish to occupy, is waiting for you, and your man is still there. As you were never publicly accused, we considered that there was no need of a public exculpation. But on that, of course, you must please yourself.'

'We may want your assistance later on, MacGillivray,' Sir Walter said as we left.

Then he turned me loose.

'Come and see me to-morrow, Hannay. I needn't tell you to keep deadly quiet. If I were you I would go to bed, for you must have considerable arrears of sleep to overtake. You had better lie low, for if one of your Black Stone friends saw you there might be trouble.'

I felt curiously at a loose end. At first it was very pleasant to be a free man, able to go where I wanted without fearing anything. I had only been a month under the ban of the law, and it was quite enough for me. I went to the Savoy and ordered very carefully a very good luncheon, and then smoked the best cigar the house could provide. But I was still feeling nervous. When I saw anybody look at me in the lounge, I grew shy, and wondered if they were thinking about the murder.

After that I took a taxi and drove miles away up into North London. I walked back through fields and lines of villas and terraces and then slums and mean streets, and it took me pretty nearly two hours. All the while my restlessness was growing worse. I felt that great things, tremendous things, were happening or about to happen, and I, who was the cog-wheel of the whole business, was out of it. Royer would be landing at Dover, Sir Walter would be making plans with the few people in England who were in the secret, and somewhere in the darkness the Black Stone would be working. I felt the sense of danger and impending calamity, and I had the curious feeling, too, that I alone could avert it, alone could grapple with it. But I was out of the game now. How could it be otherwise? It was not likely that Cabinet Ministers and Admiralty Lords and Generals would admit me to their councils.

I actually began to wish that I could run up against one of my three enemies. That would lead to developments. I felt that I wanted enormously to have a vulgar scrap with those gentry, where I could hit out and flatten something. I was rapidly getting into a very bad temper.

I didn't feel like going back to my flat. That had to be faced some time, but as I still had sufficient money I thought I would put it off till next morning, and go to a hotel for the night.

My irritation lasted through dinner, which I had at a restaurant in Jermyn Street. I was no longer hungry, and let several courses pass untasted. I drank the best part of a bottle of Burgundy, but it did nothing to cheer me. An abominable restlessness had taken possession of me. Here was I, a very ordinary fellow, with no particular brains, and yet I was convinced that somehow I was needed to help this business through – that without me it would all go to blazes. I told myself it was sheer silly conceit, that four or five of the cleverest people living, with all the might of the British Empire at their back, had the job in hand. Yet I couldn't be convinced. It seemed as if a voice kept speaking in my ear, telling me to be up and doing, or I would never sleep again.

The upshot was that about half-past nine I made up my mind to go to Queen Anne's Gate. Very likely I would not be admitted, but it would ease my conscience to try.

I walked down Jermyn Street, and at the corner of Duke Street passed a group of young men. They were in evening dress, had been dining somewhere, and were going on to a music-hall. One of them was Mr Marmaduke Jopley.

He saw me and stopped short.

'By God, the murderer!' he cried. 'Here, you fellows, hold him! That's Hannay, the man who did the Portland Place murder!' He gripped me by the arm, and the others crowded round.

I wasn't looking for any trouble, but my ill-temper made me play the fool. A policeman came up, and I should have told him the truth, and, if he didn't believe it, demanded to be taken to Scotland Yard, or for that matter to the nearest police station. But a delay at that moment seemed to me unendurable, and the sight of Marmie's imbecile face was more than I could bear. I let out with my left, and had the satisfaction of seeing him measure his length in the gutter.

Then began an unholy row. They were all on me at once, and the policeman took me in the rear. I got in one or two good blows, for I think, with fair play, I could have licked the lot of them, but the policeman pinned me behind, and one of them got his fingers on my throat.

Through a black cloud of rage I heard the officer of the law asking what was the matter, and Marmie, between his broken teeth, declaring that I was Hannay the murderer.

'Oh, damn it all,' I cried, 'make the fellow shut up. I advise you to leave me alone, constable. Scotland Yard knows all about me, and you'll get a proper wigging if you interfere with me.'

'You've got to come along of me, young man,' said the policeman. 'I saw you strike that gentleman crool 'ard. You began it too, for he wasn't doing nothing. I seen you. Best go quietly or I'll have to fix you up.'

Exasperation and an overwhelming sense that at no cost must I delay gave me the strength of a bull elephant. I fairly wrenched the constable off his feet, floored the man who was gripping my collar, and set off at my best pace down Duke Street. I heard a whistle being blown, and the rush of men behind me.

I have a very fair turn of speed, and that night I had wings. In a jiffey I was in Pall Mall and had turned down towards St James's

Park. I dodged the policeman at the Palace gates, dived through a press of carriages at the entrance to the Mall, and was making for the bridge before my pursuers had crossed the roadway. In the open ways of the Park I put on a spurt. Happily there were few people about and no one tried to stop me. I was staking all on getting to Queen Anne's Gate.

When I entered that quiet thoroughfare it seemed deserted. Sir Walter's house was in the narrow part, and outside it three or four motor-cars were drawn up. I slackened speed some yards off and walked briskly up to the door. If the butler refused me admission, or if he even delayed to open the door, I was done.

He didn't delay. I had scarcely rung before the door opened.

'I must see Sir Walter,' I panted. 'My business is desperately important.'

That butler was a great man. Without moving a muscle he held the door open, and then shut it behind me. 'Sir Walter is engaged, sir, and I have orders to admit no one. Perhaps you will wait.'

The house was of the old-fashioned kind, with a wide hall and rooms on both sides of it. At the far end was an alcove with a telephone and a couple of chairs, and there the butler offered me a seat.

'See here,' I whispered. 'There's trouble about and I'm in it. But Sir Walter knows, and I'm working for him. If any one comes and asks if I am here, tell him a lie.'

He nodded, and presently there was a noise of voices in the street, and a furious ringing at the bell. I never admired a man more than that butler. He opened the door, and with a face like a graven image waited to be questioned. Then he gave them it. He told them whose house it was, and what his orders were, and simply froze them off the doorstep. I could see it all from my alcove, and it was better than any play.

I hadn't waited long till there came another ring at the bell. The butler made no bones about admitting this new visitor.

While he was taking off his coat I saw who it was. You couldn't open a newspaper or a magazine without seeing that face – the grey beard cut like a spade, the firm fighting mouth, the blunt square nose, and the keen blue eyes. I recognised the First Sea Lord,[3] the man, they say, that made the new British Navy.

He passed my alcove and was ushered into a room at the back of the hall. As the door opened I could hear the sound of low voices. It shut, and I was left alone again.

For twenty minutes I sat there, wondering what I was to do next. I was still perfectly convinced that I was wanted, but when or how I had no notion. I kept looking at my watch, and as the time crept on to half-past ten I began to think that the conference must soon end. In a quarter of an hour Royer should be speeding along the road to Portsmouth . . .

Then I heard a bell ring and the butler appeared. The door of the back room opened, and the First Sea Lord came out. He walked past me, and in passing he glanced in my direction, and for a second we looked each other in the face.

Only for a second, but it was enough to make my heart jump. I had never seen the great man before, and he had never seen me. But in that fraction of time something sprang into his eyes, and that something was recognition. You can't mistake it. It is a flicker, a spark of light, a minute shade of difference which means one thing and one thing only. It came involuntarily, for in a moment it died, and he passed on. In a maze of wild fancies I heard the street door close behind him.

I picked up the telephone book and looked up the number of his house. We were connected at once, and I heard a servant's voice.

'Is his Lordship at home?' I asked.

'His Lordship returned half an hour ago,' said the voice, 'and has gone to bed. He is not very well to-night. Will you leave a message, sir?'

I rung off and almost tumbled into a chair. My part in this business was not yet ended. It had been a close shave, but I had been in time.

Not a moment could be lost, so I marched boldly to the door of that back room and entered without knocking. Five surprised faces looked up from a round table. There was Sir Walter, and Drew the War Minister, whom I knew from his photographs.

There was a slim elderly man, who was probably Whittaker, the Admiralty official, and there was General Winstanley, conspicuous from the long scar on his forehead. Lastly, there was a short stout man with an iron-grey moustache and bushy eyebrows, who had been arrested in the middle of a sentence.

Sir Walter's face showed surprise and annoyance.

'This is Mr Hannay, of whom I have spoken to you,' he said apologetically to the company. 'I'm afraid, Hannay, this visit is ill-timed.'

I was getting back my coolness. 'That remains to be seen, sir,' I said; 'but I think it may be in the nick of time. For God's sake, gentlemen, tell me who went out a minute ago?'

'Lord Alloa,' Sir Walter said, reddening with anger.

'It was not,' I cried; 'it was his living image, but it was not Lord Alloa. It was some one who recognised me, some one I have seen in the last month. He had scarcely left the doorstep when I rang up Lord Alloa's house and was told he had come in half an hour before and had gone to bed.'

'Who – who–' some one stammered.

'The Black Stone,' I cried, and I sat down in the chair so recently vacated and looked round at five badly scared gentlemen.

CHAPTER IX
THE THIRTY-NINE STEPS

'Nonsense!' said the official from the Admiralty.

Sir Walter got up and left the room while we looked blankly at the table. He came back in ten minutes with a long face. 'I have spoken to Alloa,' he said. 'Had him out of bed – very grumpy. He went straight home after Mulross's dinner.'

'But it's madness,' broke in General Winstanley. 'Do you mean to tell me that that man came here and sat beside me for the best part of half an hour and that I didn't detect the imposture? Alloa must be out of his mind.'

'Don't you see the cleverness of it?' I said. 'You were too interested in other things to have any eyes. You took Lord Alloa for granted. If it had been anybody else you might have looked more closely, but it was natural for him to be here, and that put you all to sleep.'

Then the Frenchman spoke, very slowly and in good English.

'The young man is right. His psychology is good. Our enemies have not been foolish!'

He bent his wise brows on the assembly.

'I will tell you a tale,' he said. 'It happened many years ago in Senegal.[1] I was quartered in a remote station, and to pass the time used to go fishing for big barbel in the river. A little Arab mare used to carry my luncheon basket – one of the salted dun breed you got at Timbuctoo in the old days. Well, one morning I had good sport, and the mare was unaccountably restless. I could hear her whinnying and squealing and stamping her feet, and I kept soothing her with my voice while my mind was intent on fish. I could see her all the time, as I thought, out of a corner of my eye, tethered to a tree twenty yards away ... After a couple of hours I began to think of food. I collected my fish in a tarpaulin bag, and moved down the stream towards the mare, trolling my line. When I got up to her I flung the tarpaulin on her back . . .'

He paused and looked round.

'It was the smell that gave me warning. I turned my head and found myself looking at a lion three feet off . . . An old man-eater, that was the terror of the village . . . What was left of the mare, a mass of blood and bones and hide, was behind him.'

'What happened?' I asked. I was enough of a hunter to know a true yarn when I heard it.

'I stuffed my fishing-rod into his jaws, and I had a pistol. Also my servants came presently with rifles. But he left his mark on me.' He held up a hand which lacked three fingers.

'Consider,' he said. 'The mare had been dead more than an hour, and the brute had been patiently watching me ever since. I never saw the kill, for I was accustomed to the mare's fretting, and I never marked her absence, for my consciousness of her was only of something tawny, and the lion filled that part. If I could blunder thus, gentlemen, in a land where men's senses are keen, why should we busy preoccupied urban folk not err also?'

Sir Walter nodded. No one was ready to gainsay him.

'But I don't see,' went on Winstanley. 'Their object was to get these dispositions without our knowing it. Now it only required one of us to mention to Alloa our meeting to-night for the whole fraud to be exposed.'

Sir Walter laughed dryly. 'The selection of Alloa shows their acumen. Which of us was likely to speak to him about to-night? Or was he likely to open the subject?'

I remembered the First Sea Lord's reputation for taciturnity and shortness of temper.

'The one thing that puzzles me,' said the General, 'is what good his visit here would do that spy fellow? He could not carry away several pages of figures and strange names in his head.'

'That is not difficult,' the Frenchman replied. 'A good spy is trained to have a photographic memory. Like your own Macaulay.[2] You noticed he said nothing, but went through these papers again and again. I think we may assume that he has every detail stamped on his mind. When I was younger I could do the same trick.'

'Well, I suppose there is nothing for it but to change the plans,' said Sir Walter ruefully.

Whittaker was looking very glum. 'Did you tell Lord Alloa what has happened?' he asked. 'No? Well, I can't speak with absolute assurance, but I'm nearly certain we can't make any serious change unless we alter the geography of England.'

'Another thing must be said,' it was Royer who spoke. 'I talked freely when that man was here. I told something of the military plans of my Government. I was permitted to say so much. But that information would be worth many millions to our enemies. No, my friends, I see no other way. The man who came here and his confederates must be taken, and taken at once.'

'Good God,' I cried, 'and we have not a rag of a clue.'

'Besides,' said Whittaker, 'there is the post. By this time the news will be on its way.'

'No,' said the Frenchman. 'You do not understand the habits of the spy. He receives personally his reward, and he delivers personally his intelligence. We in France know something of the breed. There is still a chance, *mes amis*. These men must cross the sea, and there are ships to be searched and ports to be watched. Believe me, the need is desperate for both France and Britain.'

Royer's grave good sense seemed to pull us together. He was the man of action among fumblers. But I saw no hope in any face, and I felt none. Where among the fifty millions of these islands and within a dozen hours were we to lay hands on the three cleverest rogues in Europe?

Then suddenly I had an inspiration.

'Where is Scudder's book?' I cried to Sir Walter. 'Quick, man, I remember something in it.'

He unlocked the door of a bureau and gave it to me.

I found the place. '*Thirty-nine steps*,' I read, and again, '*Thirty-nine steps – I counted them – High tide*, 10.17 P.M.'

The Admiralty man was looking at me as if he thought I had gone mad.

'Don't you see it's a clue,' I shouted. 'Scudder knew where these fellows laired – he knew where they were going to leave the country, though he kept the name to himself. To-morrow was the day, and it was some place where high tide was at 10.17.'

'They may have gone to-night,' some one said.

'Not they. They have their own snug secret way, and they won't be hurried. I know Germans, and they are mad about working to a plan. Where the devil can I get a book of Tide Tables?'

Whittaker brightened up. 'It's a chance,' he said. 'Let's go over to the Admiralty.'

We got into two of the waiting motor-cars – all but Sir Walter, who went off to Scotland Yard – to 'mobilise MacGillivray,' so he said.

We marched through empty corridors and big bare chambers where the char-women were busy, till we reached a little room lined with books and maps. A resident clerk was unearthed, who presently fetched from the library the Admiralty Tide Tables. I sat at the desk and the others stood round, for somehow or other I had got charge of this expedition.

It was no good. There were hundreds of entries, and so far as I could see 10.17 might cover fifty places. We had to find some way of narrowing the possibilities.

I took my head in my hands and thought. There must be some way of reading this riddle. What did Scudder mean by steps? I thought of dock steps, but if he had meant that I didn't think he would have mentioned the number. It must be some place where there were several staircases, and one marked out from the others by having thirty-nine steps.

Then I had a sudden thought, and hunted up all the steamer sailings. There was no boat which left for the Continent at 10.17 P.M.

Why was high tide important? If it was a harbour it must be some little place where the tide mattered, or else it was a heavy-draught boat. But there was no regular steamer sailing at that hour, and somehow I didn't think they would travel by a big boat from a regular harbour. So it must be some little harbour where the tide was important, or perhaps no harbour at all.

But if it was a little port I couldn't see what the steps signified. There were no sets of staircases on any harbour that I had ever seen. It must be some place which a particular staircase identified, and where the tide was full at 10.17. On the whole it seemed to me that the place must be a bit of open coast. But the staircases kept puzzling me.

Then I went back to wider considerations. Whereabouts would a man be likely to leave for Germany, a man in a hurry, who wanted a speedy and a secret passage? Not from any of the big harbours. And not from the Channel or the West Coast or Scotland, for, remember, he was starting from London. I measured the distance on the map, and tried to put myself in the enemy's shoes. I should try for Ostend or Antwerp or Rotterdam, and I should sail from somewhere on the East Coast between Cromer and Dover.

All this was very loose guessing, and I don't pretend it was ingenious or scientific. I wasn't any kind of Sherlock Holmes. But I have always fancied I had a kind of instinct about questions like this. I don't know if I can explain myself, but I used to use my brains as far as they went, and after they came to a blank wall I guessed, and I usually found my guesses pretty right.

So I set out all my conclusions on a bit of Admiralty paper. They ran like this:—

Fairly Certain

(1) Place where there are several sets of stairs; one that matters distinguished by having thirty-nine steps.
(2) Full tide at 10.17 P.M. Leaving shore only possible at full tide.
(3) Steps not dock steps, and so place probably not harbour.
(4) No regular night steamer at 10.17. Means of transport must be tramp (unlikely), yacht, or fishing-boat.

There my reasoning stopped. I made another list, which I headed 'Guessed,' but I was just as sure of the one as the other.

Guessed

(1) Place not harbour but open coast.
(2) Boat small – trawler, yacht, or launch.
(3) Place somewhere on East Coast between Cromer and Dover.

It struck me as odd that I should be sitting at that desk with a Cabinet Minister, a Field-Marshal, two high Government officials, and a French General watching me, while from the scribble of a dead man I was trying to drag a secret which meant life or death for us.

Sir Walter had joined us, and presently MacGillivray arrived. He had sent out instructions to watch the ports and railway stations for the three men whom I had described to Sir Walter. Not that he or anybody else thought that that would do much good.

'Here's the most I can make of it,' I said. 'We have got to find a place where there are several staircases down to the beach, one of which has thirty-nine steps. I think it's a piece of open coast with biggish cliffs, somewhere between the Wash and the Channel. Also it's a place where full tide is at 10.17 to-morrow night.'

Then an idea struck me. 'Is there no Inspector of Coastguards or some fellow like that who knows the East Coast?'

Whittaker said there was, and that he lived in Clapham. He went off in a car to fetch him, and the rest of us sat about the little room and talked of anything that came into our heads. I lit a pipe and went over the whole thing again till my brain grew weary.

About one in the morning the coastguard man arrived. He was a fine old fellow, with the look of a naval officer, and was desperately respectful to the company. I left the War Minister to cross-examine him, for I felt he would think it cheek in me to talk.

'We want you to tell us the places you know on the East Coast where there are cliffs, and where several sets of steps run down to the beach.'

He thought for a bit. 'What kind of steps do you mean, sir?

There are plenty of places with roads cut down through the cliffs, and most roads have a step or two in them. Or do you mean regular staircases – all steps, so to speak?'

Sir Arthur looked towards me. 'We mean regular staircases,' I said.

He reflected a minute or two. 'I don't know that I can think of any. Wait a second. There's a place in Norfolk – Brattlesham – beside a golf course, where there are a couple of staircases to let the gentlemen get a lost ball.'

'That's not it,' I said.

'Then there are plenty of Marine Parades, if that's what you mean. Every seaside resort has them.'

I shook my head.

'It's got to be more retired than that,' I said.

'Well, gentlemen, I can't think of anywhere else. Of course, there's the Ruff —'

'What's that?' I asked.

'The big chalk headland in Kent, close to Bradgate. It's got a lot of villas on the top, and some of the houses have staircases down to a private beach. It's a very high-toned sort of place, and the residents there like to keep by themselves.'

I tore open the Tide Tables and found Bradgate. High tide there was at 10.27 P.M. on the 15th of June.

'We're on the scent at last,' I cried excitedly. 'How can I find out what is the tide at the Ruff?'

'I can tell you that, sir,' said the coastguard man. 'I once was lent a house there in this very month, and I used to go out at night to the deep-sea fishing. The tide's ten minutes before Bradgate.'

I closed the book and looked round at the company.

'If one of those staircases has thirty-nine steps we have solved the mystery, gentlemen,' I said. 'I want the loan of your car, Sir Walter, and a map of the roads. If Mr MacGillivray will spare me ten minutes, I think we can prepare something for to-morrow.'

It was ridiculous in me to take charge of the business like this, but they didn't seem to mind, and after all I had been in the show from the start. Besides, I was used to rough jobs, and these eminent gentlemen were too clever not to see it. It was General

Royer who gave me my commission. 'I for one,' he said, 'am content to leave the matter in Mr Hannay's hands.'

By half-past three I was tearing past the moonlit hedgerows of Kent, with MacGillivray's best man on the seat beside me.

CHAPTER X
VARIOUS PARTIES CONVERGING ON THE SEA

A pink and blue June morning found me at Bradgate looking from the Griffin Hotel over a smooth sea to the lightship on the Cock sands which seemed the size of a bell-buoy. A couple of miles farther south and much nearer the shore a small destroyer was anchored. Scaife, MacGillivray's man, who had been in the Navy, knew the boat, and told me her name and her commander's, so I sent off a wire to Sir Walter.

After breakfast Scaife got from a house-agent a key for the gates of the staircases on the Ruff. I walked with him along the sands, and sat down in a nook of the cliffs while he investigated the half dozen of them. I didn't want to be seen, but the place at this hour was quite deserted, and all the time I was on that beach I saw nothing but the sea-gulls.

It took him more than an hour to do the job, and when I saw him coming towards me, conning a bit of paper, I can tell you my heart was in my mouth. Everything depended, you see, on my guess proving right.

He read aloud the number of steps in the different stairs. 'Thirty-four, thirty-five, thirty-nine, forty-two, forty-seven,' and 'twenty-one' where the cliffs grew lower. I almost got up and shouted.

We hurried back to the town and sent a wire to MacGillivray. I wanted half a dozen men, and I directed them to divide themselves among different specified hotels. Then Scaife set out to prospect the house at the head of the thirty-nine steps.

He came back with news that both puzzled and reassured me. The house was called Trafalgar Lodge, and belonged to an old gentleman called Appleton – a retired stockbroker, the house-agent said. Mr Appleton was there a good deal in the summer time, and was in residence now – had been for the better part of a week. Scaife could pick up very little information about him, except that he was a decent old fellow, who paid his bills regularly, and was always good for a fiver for a local charity. Then Scaife seems to have penetrated to the back-door of the house, pretending he was an agent for sewing-machines. Only three servants were kept, a cook, a parlour-maid, and a house-maid, and they were just the sort that you would find in a respectable middle-class household. The cook was not the gossiping kind, and had pretty soon shut the door in his face, but Scaife said he was positive she knew nothing. Next door there was a new house building which would give good cover for observation, and the villa on the other side was to let, and its garden was rough and shrubby.

I borrowed Scaife's telescope, and before lunch went for a walk along the Ruff. I kept well behind the rows of villas, and found a good observation point on the edge of the golf-course. There I had a view of the line of turf along the cliff top, with seats placed at intervals, and the little square plots, railed in and planted with bushes, whence the staircases descended to the beach. I saw Trafalgar Lodge very plainly, a red-brick villa with a verandah, a tennis lawn behind, and in front the ordinary seaside flower-garden full of marguerites and scraggy gera-niums. There was a flagstaff from which an enormous Union Jack hung limply in the still air.

Presently I observed some one leave the house and saunter along the cliff. When I got my glasses on him I saw it was an old man, wearing white flannel trousers, a blue serge jacket, and a straw hat. He carried field-glasses and a newspaper, and sat down on one of the iron seats and began to read. Sometimes he would lay down the paper and turn his glasses on the sea. He looked for a long time at the destroyer. I watched him for half an hour, till he got up and went back to the house for his luncheon, when I returned to the hotel for mine.

I wasn't feeling very confident. This decent commonplace dwelling was not what I had expected. The man might be the bald archaeologist of that horrible moorland farm, or he might not. He was exactly the kind of satisfied old bird you will find in every suburb and every holiday place. If you wanted a type of the perfectly harmless person you would probably pitch on that.

But after lunch, as I sat in the hotel porch, I perked up, for I saw the thing I had hoped for and had dreaded to miss. A yacht came up from the south and dropped anchor pretty well opposite the Ruff. She seemed about a hundred and fifty tons and I saw she belonged to the Squadron[1] from the white ensign. So Scaife and I went down to the harbour and hired a boatman for an afternoon's fishing.

I spent a warm and peaceful afternoon. We caught between us about twenty pounds of cod and lythe, and out in that dancing blue sea I took a cheerier view of things. Above the white cliffs of the Ruff I saw the green and red of the villas, and especially the great flagstaff of Trafalgar Lodge. About four o'clock, when we had fished enough, I made the boatman row us round the yacht, which lay like a delicate white bird, ready at a moment to flee. Scaife said she must be a fast boat from her build, and that she was pretty heavily engined.

Her name was the *Ariadne*, as I discovered from the cap of one of the men who was polishing brasswork. I spoke to him, and got an answer in the soft dialect of Essex. Another hand that came along passed me the time of day in an unmistakable English tongue. Our boatman had an argument with one of them about the weather, and for a few minutes we lay on our oars close to the starboard bow.

Then the men suddenly disregarded us and bent their heads to their work as an officer came along the deck. He was a pleasant, clean-looking young fellow, and he put a question to us about our fishing in very good English. But there could be no doubt about him. His close-cropped head and the cut of his collar and tie never came out of England.

That did something to reassure me, but as we rowed back to Bradgate my obstinate doubts would not be dismissed. The thing that worried me was the reflection that my enemies knew that I had got my knowledge from Scudder, and it was Scudder who had given me the clue to this place. If they knew that

Scudder had this clue, would they not be certain to change their plans? Too much depended on their success for them to take any risks. The whole question was how much they understood about Scudder's knowledge. I had talked confidently last night about Germans always sticking to a scheme, but if they had any suspicions that I was on their track they would be fools not to cover it. I wondered if the man last night had seen that I recognised him. Somehow I did not think he had, and to that I clung. But the whole business had never seemed so difficult as that afternoon when by all calculations I should have been rejoicing in assured success.

In the hotel I met the commander of the destroyer, to whom Scaife introduced me, and with whom I had a few words. Then I thought I would put in an hour or two watching Trafalgar Lodge.

I found a place farther up the hill, in the garden of an empty house. From there I had a full view of the court, on which two figures were having a game of tennis. One was the old man, whom I had already seen; the other was a younger fellow, wearing some club colours in the scarf round his middle. They played with tremendous zest, like two city gents who wanted hard exercise to open their pores. You couldn't conceive a more innocent spectacle. They shouted and laughed and stopped for drinks, when a maid brought out two tankards on a salver. I rubbed my eyes and asked myself if I was not the most immortal fool on earth. Mystery and darkness had hung about the men who hunted me over the Scotch moor in aeroplane and motorcar, and notably about that infernal antiquarian. It was easy enough to connect those folk with the knife that pinned Scudder to the floor, and with fell designs on the world's peace. But here were two guileless citizens taking their innocuous exercise, and soon about to go indoors to a humdrum dinner, where they would talk of market prices and the last cricket scores and the gossip of their native Surbiton. I had been making a net to catch vultures and falcons, and lo and behold! two plump thrushes had blundered into it.

Presently a third figure arrived, a young man on a bicycle, with a bag of golf-clubs slung on his back. He strolled round to the tennis lawn and was welcomed riotously by the players. Evidently they were chaffing him, and their chaff sounded horribly English. Then the plump man, mopping his brow with a silk handkerchief, announced that he must have a tub. I heard his very words – 'I've got into a proper lather,' he said. 'This will bring down my weight and my handicap, Bob. I'll take you on to-morrow and give you a stroke a hole.' You couldn't find anything much more English than that.

They all went into the house, and left me feeling a precious idiot. I had been barking up the wrong tree this time. These men might be acting; but if they were, where was their audience? They didn't know I was sitting thirty yards off in a rhododendron. It was simply impossible to believe that these three hearty fellows were anything but what they seemed – three ordinary, game-playing, suburban Englishmen, wearisome, if you like, but sordidly innocent.

And yet there were three of them; and one was old, and one was plump, and one was lean and dark; and their house chimed in with Scudder's notes; and half a mile off was lying a steam yacht with at least one German officer. I thought of Karolides lying dead and all Europe trembling on the edge of earthquake, and the men I had left behind me in London who were waiting anxiously for the events of the next hours. There was no doubt that hell was afoot somewhere. The Black Stone had won, and if it survived this June night would bank its winnings.

There seemed only one thing to do – go forward as if I had no doubts, and if I was going to make a fool of myself to do it handsomely. Never in my life have I faced a job with greater disinclination. I would rather in my then mind have walked into a den of anarchists, each with his Browning[2] handy, or faced a charging lion with a popgun, than enter that happy home of three cheerful Englishmen and tell them that their game was up. How they would laugh at me!

But suddenly I remembered a thing I once heard in Rhodesia from old Peter Pienaar. I have quoted Peter already in this narrative. He was the best scout I ever knew, and before he had turned respectable he had been pretty often on the windy side of the law, when he had been wanted badly by the authorities. Peter once discussed with me the question of disguises, and he had a theory which struck me at the time. He said, barring absolute certainties like fingerprints, mere physical traits were very little use for identification if the fugitive really knew his business. He laughed at things like dyed hair and false beards and such childish follies. The only thing that mattered was what Peter called 'ammosphere.'

If a man could get into perfectly different surroundings from those in which he had been first observed, and – this is the important part – really play up to these surroundings and behave as if he had never been out of them, he would puzzle the cleverest detectives on earth. And he used to tell a story of how he once borrowed a black coat and went to church and shared the same hymn-book with the man that was looking for him. If that man had seen him in decent company before he would have recognised him; but he had only seen him snuffing the lights in a public-house with a revolver.

The recollection of Peter's talk gave me the first real comfort I had had that day. Peter had been a wise old bird, and these fellows I was after were about the pick of the aviary. What if they were playing Peter's game? A fool tries to look different: a clever man looks the same and *is* different.

Again, there was that other maxim of Peter's, which had helped me when I had been a roadman. 'If you are playing a part, you will never keep it up unless you convince yourself that you are *it*.' That would explain the game of tennis. Those chaps didn't need to act, they just turned a handle and passed into another life, which came as naturally to them as the first. It sounds a platitude, but Peter used to say that it was the big secret of all the famous criminals.

It was now getting on for eight o'clock, and I went back and saw Scaife to give him his instructions. I arranged with him how to place his men, and then I went for a walk, for I didn't feel up to any dinner. I went round the deserted golf-course, and then to a point on the cliffs farther north beyond the line of the villas. On the little trim newly-made roads I met people in flannels coming back from tennis and the beach, and a coastguard from the wireless station, and donkeys and pierrots padding homewards. Out at sea in the blue dusk I saw lights appear on the *Ariadne* and on the destroyer away to the south, and beyond the Cock sands the bigger lights of steamers making for the Thames. The whole scene was so peaceful and ordinary that I got more dashed in spirits every second. It took all my resolution to stroll towards Trafalgar Lodge about half-past nine.

On the way I got a piece of solid comfort from the sight of a greyhound that was swinging along at a nursemaid's heels. He reminded me of a dog I used to have in Rhodesia, and of the time when I took him hunting with me in the Pali hills. We were after rhebok,[3] the dun kind, and I recollected how we had followed one beast, and both he and I had clean lost it. A greyhound works by sight, and my eyes are good enough, but that buck simply leaked out of the landscape. Afterwards I found out how it managed it. Against the grey rock of the kopjes it showed no more than a crow against a thundercloud. It didn't need to run away; all it had to do was to stand still and melt into the background.

Suddenly as these memories chased across my brain I thought of my present case and applied the moral. The Black Stone didn't need to bolt. They were quietly absorbed into the landscape. I was on the right track, and I jammed that down in my mind and vowed never to forget it. The last word was with Peter Pienaar.

Scaife's men would be posted now, but there was no sign of a soul. The house stood as open as a market-place for anybody to observe. A three-foot railing separated it from the cliff road; the windows on the ground-floor were all open, and shaded lights and the low sound of voices revealed where the occupants were finishing dinner. Everything was as public and above-board as a charity bazaar. Feeling the greatest fool on earth, I opened the gate and rang the bell.

A man of my sort, who has travelled about the world in rough places, gets on perfectly well with two classes, what you may call the upper and the lower. He understands them and they understand him. I was at home with herds and tramps and roadmen, and I was sufficiently at my ease with people like Sir

Walter and the men I had met the night before. I can't explain why, but it is a fact. But what fellows like me don't understand is the great comfortable, satisfied middle-class world, the folk that live in villas and suburbs. He doesn't know how they look at things, he doesn't understand their conventions, and he is as shy of them as of a black mamba.[4] When a trim parlour-maid opened the door, I could hardly find my voice.

I asked for Mr Appleton, and was ushered in. My plan had been to walk straight into the dining-room, and by a sudden appearance wake in the men that start of recognition which would confirm my theory. But when I found myself in that neat hall the place mastered me. There were the golf-clubs and tennis-rackets, the straw hats and caps, the rows of gloves, the sheaf of walking-sticks, which you will find in ten thousand British homes. A stack of neatly folded coats and waterproofs covered the top of an old oak chest; there was a grandfather clock ticking; and some polished brass warming-pans on the walls, and a barometer, and a print of Chiltern winning the St Leger. The place was as orthodox as an Anglican church. When the maid asked me for my name I gave it automatically, and was shown into the smoking-room, on the right side of the hall.

That room was even worse. I hadn't time to examine it, but I could see some framed group photographs above the mantelpiece, and I could have sworn they were English public school or college. I had only one glance, for I managed to pull myself together and go after the maid. But I was too late. She had already entered the dining-room and given my name to her master, and I had missed the chance of seeing how the three took it.

When I walked into the room the old man at the head of the table had risen and turned round to meet me. He was in evening dress – a short coat and black tie, as was the other, whom I called in my own mind the plump one. The third, the dark fellow, wore a blue serge suit and a soft white collar, and the colours of some club or school.

The old man's manner was perfect. 'Mr Hannay?' he said hesitatingly. 'Did you wish to see me? One moment, you fellows, and I'll rejoin you. We had better go to the smoking-room.'

Though I hadn't an ounce of confidence in me, I forced myself to play the game. I pulled up a chair and sat down on it.

'I think we have met before,' I said, 'and I guess you know my business.'

The light in the room was dim, but so far as I could see their faces, they played the part of mystification very well.

'Maybe, maybe,' said the old man. 'I haven't a very good memory, but I'm afraid you must tell me your errand, sir, for I really don't know it.'

'Well, then,' I said, and all the time I seemed to myself to be talking pure foolishness – 'I have come to tell you that the game's up. I have here a warrant for the arrest of you three gentlemen.'

'Arrest,' said the old man, and he looked really shocked. 'Arrest! Good God, what for?'

'For the murder of Franklin Scudder in London on the 23rd day of last month.'

'I never heard the name before,' said the old man in a dazed voice.

One of the others spoke up. 'That was the Portland Place murder. I read about it. Good heavens, you must be mad, sir! Where do you come from?'

'Scotland Yard,' I said.

After that for a minute there was utter silence. The old man was staring at his plate and fumbling with a nut, the very model of innocent bewilderment.

Then the plump one spoke up. He stammered a little, like a man picking his words.

'Don't get flustered, uncle,' he said. 'It is all a ridiculous mistake; but these things happen sometimes, and we can easily set it right. It won't be hard to prove our innocence. I can show that I was out of the country on the 23rd of May, and Bob was in a nursing-home. You were in London, but you can explain what you were doing.'

'Right, Percy! Of course that's easy enough. The 23rd! That was the day after Agatha's wedding. Let me see. What was I doing? I came up in the morning from Woking, and lunched at the Club with Charlie Symons. Then – oh yes, I dined with the Fishmongers.[5] I remember, for the punch didn't agree with me, and I was seedy next morning. Hang it all, there's the cigar-box I brought back from the dinner.' He pointed to an object on the table, and laughed nervously.

'I think, sir,' said the young man, addressing me respectfully, 'you will see you are mistaken. We want to assist the law like all Englishmen, and we don't want Scotland Yard to be making fools of themselves. That's so, uncle?'

'Certainly, Bob.' The old fellow seemed to be recovering his voice. 'Certainly, we'll do anything in our power to assist the authorities. But – but this is a bit too much. I can't get over it.'

'How Nellie will chuckle,' said the plump man. 'She always said that you would die of boredom because nothing ever happened to you. And now you've got it thick and strong,' and he began to laugh very pleasantly.

'By Jove, yes. Just think of it! What a story to tell at the club. Really, Mr Hannay, I suppose I should be angry, to show my innocence, but it's too funny! I almost forgive you the fright you gave me! You looked so glum, I thought I might have been walking in my sleep and killing people.'

It couldn't be acting, it was too confoundedly genuine. My heart went into my boots, and my first impulse was to apologise and clear out. But I told myself I must see it through, even though I was to be the laughing-stock of Britain. The light from the dinner-table candlesticks was not very good, and to cover my confusion I got up, walked to the door and switched on the electric light. The sudden glare made them blink, and I stood scanning the three faces.

Well, I made nothing of it. One was old and bald, one was stout, one was dark and thin. There was nothing in their appearance to prevent them being the three who had hunted me in Scotland, but there was nothing to identify them. I simply can't explain why I who, as a roadman, had looked into two pair of eyes, and as Ned Ainslie into another pair, why I, who have a good memory and reasonable powers of observation, could find no satisfaction. They seemed exactly what they professed to be, and I could not have sworn to one of them.

There in that pleasant dining-room, with etchings on the walls, and a picture of an old lady in a bib above the mantelpiece,

I could see nothing to connect them with the moorland desperadoes. There was a silver cigarette-box beside me, and I saw
that it had been won by Percival Appleton, Esq., of the St Bede's
Club, in a golf tournament. I had to keep firm hold of Peter
Pienaar to prevent myself bolting out of that house.

'Well,' said the old man politely, 'are you reassured by your
scrutiny, sir?'

I couldn't find a word.

'I hope you'll find it consistent with your duty to drop this
ridiculous business. I make no complaint, but you'll see how
annoying it must be to respectable people.'

I shook my head.

'O Lord,' said the young man. 'This is a bit too thick!'

'Do you propose to march us off to the police station?' asked
the plump one. 'That might be the best way out of it, but I
suppose you won't be content with the local branch. I have the
right to ask to see your warrant, but I don't wish to cast any
aspersions upon you. You are only doing your duty. But you'll
admit it's horribly awkward. What do you propose to do?'

There was nothing to do except to call in my men and have
them arrested, or to confess my blunder and clear out. I felt
mesmerised by the whole place, by the air of obvious innocence
– not innocence merely, but frank honest bewilderment and
concern in the three faces.

'Oh, Peter Pienaar,' I groaned inwardly, and for a moment I
was very near damning myself for a fool and asking their pardon.

'Meantime I vote we have a game of bridge,' said the plump
one. 'It will give Mr Hannay time to think over things, and you
know we have been wanting a fourth player. Do you play, sir?'

I accepted as if it had been an ordinary invitation at the club.
The whole business had mesmerised me. We went into the
smoking-room where a card-table was set out, and I was offered
things to smoke and drink. I took my place at the table in a kind
of dream. The window was open and the moon was flooding
the cliffs and sea with a great tide of yellow light. There was
moonshine, too, in my head. The three had recovered their
composure, and were talking easily – just the kind of slangy talk
you will hear in any golf club-house. I must have cut a rum

figure, sitting there knitting my brows with my eyes wandering.

My partner was the young dark one. I play a fair hand at bridge, but I must have been rank bad that night. They saw that they had got me puzzled, and that put them more than ever at their ease. I kept looking at their faces, but they conveyed nothing to me. It was not that they looked different; they *were* different. I clung desperately to the words of Peter Pienaar.

Then something awoke me.

The old man laid down his hand to light a cigar. He didn't pick it up at once, but sat back for a moment in his chair, with his fingers tapping on his knees.

It was the movement I remembered when I had stood before him in the moorland farm, with the pistols of his servants behind me.

A little thing, lasting only a second, and the odds were a thousand to one that I might have had my eyes on my cards at the time and missed it. But I didn't, and, in a flash, the air seemed to clear. Some shadow lifted from my brain, and I was looking at the three men with full and absolute recognition.

The clock on the mantelpiece struck ten o'clock.

The three faces seemed to change before my eyes and reveal their secrets. The young one was the murderer. Now I saw cruelty and ruthlessness, where before I had only seen good-humour. His knife, I made certain, had skewered Scudder to the floor. His kind had put the bullet in Karolides.

The plump man's features seemed to dislimn, and form again, as I looked at them. He hadn't a face, only a hundred masks that he could assume when he pleased. That chap must have been a superb actor. Perhaps he had been Lord Alloa of the night before; perhaps not; it didn't matter. I wondered if he was the fellow who had first tracked Scudder, and left his card on him. Scudder had said he lisped, and I could imagine how the adoption of a lisp might add terror.

But the old man was the pick of the lot. He was sheer brain, icy, cool, calculating, as ruthless as a steam hammer. Now that my eyes were opened I wondered where I had seen the benevolence. His jaw was like chilled steel, and his eyes had the inhuman luminosity of a bird's. I went on playing, and every second a greater hate welled up in my heart. It almost choked me, and I couldn't answer when my partner spoke. Only a little longer could I endure their company.

'Whew! Bob! Look at the time,' said the old man. 'You'd better think about catching your train. Bob's got to go to town to-night,' he added, turning to me. The voice rang now as false as hell.

I looked at the clock, and it was nearly half-past ten.

'I am afraid he must put off his journey,' I said.

'Oh, damn,' said the young man, 'I thought you had dropped that rot. I've simply got to go. You can have my address, and I'll give any security you like.'

'No,' I said, 'you must stay.'

At that I think they must have realised that the game was desperate. Their only chance had been to convince me that I was playing the fool, and that had failed. But the old man spoke again.

'I'll go bail for my nephew. That ought to content you, Mr Hannay.' Was it fancy, or did I detect some halt in the smoothness of that voice?

There must have been, for as I glanced at him, his eyelids fell in that hawk-like hood which fear had stamped on my memory.

I blew my whistle.

In an instant the lights were out. A pair of strong arms gripped me round the waist, covering the pockets in which a man might be expected to carry a pistol.

'Schnell, Franz,' cried a voice, 'das Boot, das Boot!'[6] As it spoke I saw two of my fellows emerge on the moonlit lawn.

The young dark man leapt for the window, was through it, and over the low fence before a hand could touch him. I grappled the old chap, and the room seemed to fill with figures. I saw the plump one collared, but my eyes were all for the out-of-doors, where Franz sped on over the road towards the railed entrance to the beach stairs. One man followed him, but he had no chance. The gate of the stairs locked behind the fugitive, and I stood staring, with my hands on the old boy's throat, for such a time as a man might take to descend those steps to the sea.

Suddenly my prisoner broke from me and flung himself on the wall. There was a click as if a lever had been pulled. Then came a low rumbling far, far below the ground, and through the window I saw a cloud of chalky dust pouring out of the shaft of the stairway.

Some one switched on the light.

The old man was looking at me with blazing eyes.

'He is safe,' he cried. 'You cannot follow in time . . . He is gone . . . He has triumphed . . . *Der Schwarzestein ist in der Siegeskrone.*'[7]

There was more in those eyes than any common triumph. They had been hooded like a bird of prey, and now they flamed with a hawk's pride. A white fanatic heat burned in them, and I realised for the first time the terrible thing I had been up against. This man was more than a spy; in his foul way he had been a patriot.

As the handcuffs clinked on his wrists I said my last word to him.

'I hope Franz will bear his triumph well. I ought to tell you that the *Ariadne* for the last hour has been in our hands.'

Three weeks later, as all the world knows, we went to war. I joined the New Army[8] the first week, and owing to my Matabele experience got a captain's commission straight off. But I had done my best service, I think, before I put on khaki.

THE END

Notes

CHAPTER I
THE MAN WHO DIED

1. *Buluwayo*: Mining town in Rhodesia (now Zimbabwe).
2. *pot-house*: A low drinking house.
3. *the Cape*: Of Good Hope.
4. *Langham Place*: At the top of Regent Street.
5. *things that happened in the Balkan War*: First Balkan War, 1912–13 (Bulgaria, Serbia and Greece v. Turkey); second Balkan War, 1913 (Bulgaria v. Serbia and Greece). The first was fought to reduce the size of what remained of Turkey's empire in Europe, the second over division of the spoils.
6. *pogroms*: Massacres of Jews in Czarist Russia.
7. *Mors janua vitae*: 'Death is the gateway to life'.
8. *Epirotes*: Greeks of Epirus
9. *a four-wheeler*: A horse-drawn cab.
10. *the Selakwi*: South African river.
11. *inspanned*: Employed (Afrikaans term).
12. *Blue-Grass country*: Kentucky meadow lands.

CHAPTER II
THE MILKMAN SETS OUT ON HIS TRAVELS

1. *Matabele War*: 1893.
2. *Damaraland*: Region of German South-West Africa (now Namibia).
3. *Galloway*: South-West Scotland.
4. *Bradshaw*: Railway timetable.

CHAPTER III

THE ADVENTURE OF THE LITERARY INNKEEPER

1. *Kiel*: German naval base.
2. *Delagoa Bay*: Portuguese East Africa.
3. *shag*: Cheap tobacco.
4. *the Karroo*: Arid region of Cape Province, South Africa.
5. *tarn*: Small lake.
6. *blue-ribbon*: Worn by teetotallers who had taken the pledge to abstain from strong drink.
7. *bent*: Reeds.
8. *As when a Gryphon . . . Pursues the Arimaspian*: Milton, *Paradise Lost*, Bk II, 943–5.
9. *Chambers's Journal*: Scottish literary periodical.
10. *I.D.B.*: Illicit diamond buying.
11. *the Kalahari*: South African desert.
12. *burn*: Stream.

CHAPTER IV

THE ADVENTURE OF THE RADICAL CANDIDATE

1. *Dago*: Slightly pejorative term for a Southern European male.
2. *there was a real working alliance . . . in case of war*: Staff conversations were held between the British and French armies, in secret, from 1904 to 1914.
3. *haugh*: Riverside.
4. *ulster*: Overcoat.
5. *a Free Trader*: Opposed to taxes on imports and exports.
6. *the Sixtieth*: Sixtieth Rifles (King's Royal Rifle Corps).
7. *Protection*: Taxes on foreign imports (and subsidies on domestic exports).
8. *1000-guinea car*: 1,000 guineas was worth £1,050.
9. *Henry Irving*: A leading Victorian actor.
10. *Mashona*: Rhodesian tribe.
11. *bona fides*: Latin, literally meaning 'good faith'.
12. *the Kennet*: A Berkshire trout river.

CHAPTER V

THE ADVENTURE OF THE SPECTACLED ROADMAN

1. *een*: Eyes.
2. *suckle*: Sickle.
3. *waddit*: Wedded.
4. *chiels*: People.
5. *fou*: Drunk.
6. *speir*: Question.
7. *bing o' stanes*: Heap of stones.
8. *metal*: Stone for road-making.
9. *muckle*: Big.
10. *tonneau*: Luggage container.

CHAPTER VI

THE ADVENTURE OF THE BALD ARCHAEOLOGIST

1. *Blaeberry*: Blueberry.
2. *Afrikander*: Boer.
3. *black-game*: Blackcock and blackhen.
4. *Lanchester*: Make of car.
5. *lentonite*: Blasting explosive.
6. *mill-lade*: A stream working a watermill.
7. *vol-planing*: Gliding.

CHAPTER VII

THE DRY-FLY FISHERMAN

1. *stravaigin'*: Wandering.
2. *the General Assembly*: The annual meeting of the Church of Scotland.
3. *siller*: Silver.
4. *gude-brither*: Brother-in-law.
5. *Cleuch*: Ravine.
6. *a wersh-lookin' sowl*: A feeble-looking soul.
7. *lasher*: weir.
8. *the Marineamt*: The German Admiralty.

CHAPTER VIII

THE COMING OF THE BLACK STONE

1. *the First Lord*: British Naval Minister (First Lord of the Admiralty).
2. *Sous-chef d'Etat Major-General*: Deputy Chief of the French General Staff.
3. *the First Sea Lord*: Chief of the British Naval Staff.

CHAPTER IX

THE THIRTY-NINE STEPS

1. *Senegal*: French West African colony.
2. *Macaulay*: Thomas Babington (Lord) Macaulay (1800–59) was a poet and a historian.

CHAPTER X

VARIOUS PARTIES CONVERGING ON THE SEA

1. *the Squadron*: The Royal Yacht Squadron, the leading British yacht club.
2. *Browning*: Pistol.
3. *rhebok*: Antelope.
4. *black mamba*: Snake.
5. *the Fishmongers*: City of London livery company.
6. *'Schnell, Franz . . . das Boot!'*: 'Quick, Franz . . . the boat, the boat!'
7. *'Der Schwarzestein ist in der Siegeskrone'*: 'The black stone is victorious' (literally '. . . in the victory crown').
8. *the New Army*: Volunteers raised by Field Marshal Lord Kitchener for the Great War.

THE STORY OF PENGUIN CLASSICS

Before 1946 ...'Classics' are mainly the domain of academics and students, without readable editions for everyone else. This all changes when a little-known classicist, E. V. Rieu, presents Penguin founder Allen Lane with the translation of Homer's *Odyssey* that he has been working on and reading to his wife Nelly in his spare time.

1946 *The Odyssey* becomes the first Penguin Classic published, and promptly sells three million copies. Suddenly, classic books are no longer for the privileged few.

1950s Rieu, now series editor, turns to professional writers for the best modern, readable translations, including Dorothy L. Sayers's *Inferno* and Robert Graves's *The Twelve Caesars*, which revives the salacious original.

1960s The Classics are given the distinctive black jackets that have remained a constant throughout the series's various looks. Rieu retires in 1964, hailing the Penguin Classics list as 'the greatest educative force of the 20th century'.

1970s A new generation of translators arrives to swell the Penguin Classics ranks, and the list grows to encompass more philosophy, religion, science, history and politics.

1980s The Penguin American Library joins the Classics stable, with titles such as *The Last of the Mohicans* safeguarded. Penguin Classics now offers the most comprehensive library of world literature available.

1990s The launch of Penguin Audiobooks brings the classics to a listening audience for the first time, and in 1999 the launch of the Penguin Classics website takes them online to a larger global readership than ever before.

The 21st Century Penguin Classics are rejacketed for the first time in nearly twenty years. This world famous series now consists of more than 1300 titles, making the widest range of the best books ever written available to millions – and constantly redefining the meaning of what makes a 'classic'.

The Odyssey continues ...

The best books ever written

PENGUIN CLASSICS

SINCE 1946

Find out more at www.penguinclassics.com